With Little Means

RAIMO STRANGIS

For all the dreamers

INTRODUCTION

With Little Means is a fiction novel, but that doesn't mean that everything you'll read isn't true. As far back as I can remember, music has always been a big part of my life. My mother was a huge Beatles fan, and my uncle was a drummer in a rock band. In the early nineties, we lived in a house with satellite TV. I remember watching MTV for the first time, mesmerized. When I saw the music video for Nirvana's "Smells Like Teen Spirit", I was hooked. From that moment on, I knew I wanted to be a musician. I started a band called Cranney and was living my dream. Unfortunately, not everything turned out as planned. I was diagnosed with ulcerative colitis and eventually had to end my rock star dreams. I owe a lot to music. I met my wife because of music - she was a friend of my guitarist's girlfriend, and now we have two beautiful children. I hope this novel inspires people living with a disability to never give up on their dreams. The lyrics at the end of the novel are all original songs from my days in the band.

CHAPTER ONE

My whole life I've been afraid, but I guess we all are in our own way. Most people have common fears like clowns, heights, or spiders. My fears run much deeper than that. But what scares me the most is fame. All my heroes, one by one, have been taken by the lure of fame. Kurt, Heath, Janis and Bourdain, all met their demise at the hands of fame. Some were taken by its spoils, and others by its immense pressures.

There are two things that make fame so dangerous. One, how fame is perceived, and the other, how fame is achieved. Fame has this reputation of grandeur and excitement. The lives of celebrities seem so perfect and exhilarating. We've all had posters on our bedroom walls of movie stars, athletes, and rock stars. We grow up dreaming of becoming rich and famous, just like them. But are they truly happy? Fame takes the one thing you love the most and uses it to get you. Whether your passion is music, sport, or art, it doesn't matter. Once fame finds your genius, it sucks all the love out of it and leaves you feeling empty.

I was almost famous once. I was in a kick ass indie rock band called Divine Light. We wrote great songs and played some amazing shows. But life had other plans. I got really sick and had to stop performing, and, just like that, my dream was over. Do I miss it? Of course I do. If I could go back, redo it, and go for it, would I?

What if I told you, I did, and it almost killed me.

Back in 2005, I was living my rock star dream. Writing and performing music was all I cared about; it was effortless. Our band was playing all the top venues that downtown Toronto had to offer, El Mocambo, The Reverb, Kathedral, The Horseshoe Tavern, and Lee's Palace. We even traveled to New York City and played The

Knitting Factory. Being on stage was like a drug, and I was a full-blown junkie.

After a few months on the music scene, our band started generating a little buzz. The crowds were getting larger, the gigs were getting better, and we even had a few groupies. The feeling of hundreds of people singing along with you on stage was an out of body experience. I never felt more alive; life was perfect.

It was also the beginning of social media websites like Myspace and YouTube. I was constantly checking our sites to see how many fans we had. I noticed that this one girl would always come up on our page. She would leave quirky comments and say how much she loved our songs. Finally, I decided to send her a message. We hit it off right away. The next thing I knew we were talking every day.

The first time we met in person was before one of our shows at The Reverb. It was cold out; I was standing by the front doors, smoking, shivering as she walked up with her friends. She looked just like her picture. She had beautiful green eyes, dyed red hair, and had such a great style about her - ripped jeans and a cool rock t-shirt. Time stood still. We were both so nervous.

"Hi," was all I could say.

"Hey," was all she said back.

"You look just as pretty as your picture."

"Thanks, are you nervous for your show tonight?"

"Honestly, all I could think about was meeting you. I was more nervous for that than anything. I got you something, it's in our van, wanna come with me and get it?"

"Sure, I got you something too."

I had bought her a stuffed animal, and she'd burned me a CD of all the songs that made her think of me. The one song I remember most was *Hey there, Delilah* by the Plain White Ts. We kissed for the first time. I remember it just feeling right. Love is hard to find and even harder to explain. From that point on we were inseparable.

A few months later, things started to fall apart with the band. As we got bigger, I started feeling the pressure to perform. I was constantly getting into fights with my band mates and I couldn't write a decent song if my life depended on it. Rachyl was on my mind a lot, which was never really a problem, just something new and exciting to think about. Also, I was fascinated with all these famous people dying at such a young age. I couldn't figure out why someone who had it all would do something like that? But worst of all, I started feeling sick.

It started one night at The Horseshoe Tavern, right before we had to go on stage. I was sitting on the dirty bathroom floor with my back against the stall door, clutching my stomach. I could hear the other band finishing their set. Rachyl was outside the bathroom door checking up on me. She yelled loud enough for me to hear her through the door and over the loud music.

"Rai, are you okay? The guys are calling for you, you're on next."

"I can't move, my stomach is killing me."

Once she heard that, she opened the door and walked right into the men's room with no hesitation. She found my stall and came in.

"What's wrong? What happened? Did you eat something bad? Are you nervous? What is it?"

"It's not that. I've been feeling like this for a while now; not this bad though. I thought it would just go away. I feel so nauseous. It feels like something is squeezing my guts from the inside."

"Okay, come on, you're not playing tonight, let's get you home."

I knew the guys wouldn't take this news well. This was a big show for us, and they were so excited to play that night. Rachyl started to gather her things while I went backstage to talk to the band. I opened the dressing room door and saw Maxx with his bass strapped to his shoulder, Higgins tuning his guitar, and Rikki twirling his drumsticks.

"I'm sorry, guys, I can't go tonight. I know it's a big show, but my stomach is killing me, I won't make it through the set."

"What? No, no. You're joking right? What's wrong with you."

"I wish I was, Maxx. It's my stomach, man, something's wrong. I've been in the bathroom for twenty minutes. It feels like something is stabbing me from the inside."

"The bartenders were telling me there's music reps here tonight. This could be our shot. Don't do this to us. Come on, suck it up, we're going on tonight."

"Look, man, I can barely walk, never mind playing guitar and singing. Rachyl's taking me home. I'm sorry."

Higgins and Rikki were silent. Maxx ripped off his bass in anger and said, "You do that, go home with your girlfriend. I'm going to the bar. I need a drink."

That was the last time we were ever together as a band.

My condition got so bad, I couldn't take it anymore. It was like I had the stomach flu, all day, every day. I was running to the bathroom ten times a night, and it didn't stop for a month. It's when I began to see blood in the toilet, that I finally went to see my doctor.

I remember sitting in the doctor's office with Rachyl by my side, thinking the worst.

"This is bad, Rachyl. What if it's cancer? What am I going to do."

"Stop, Rai, we don't know what it is. The doctor has the results from your biopsies. Let's not jump to any conclusions. Whatever it is, we'll get through it, okay?"

When the doctor walked in and sat at her desk, my body went numb. I took a deep breath, closed my eyes, and braced myself as she opened my file and began to read the results.

"Mr. Starings, our tests have confirmed that you have a condition called ulcerative colitis, an inflammatory disease of the large intestine. There are some options we can explore, like steroid or biologic treatments, however with your severity, I'm not sure how effective they will be."

"So, it's not cancer?"

"No, fortunately not. But I must tell you colitis is not a pleasant disease. You will face painful abdominal cramping, weight loss, fatigue, severe bleeding, and uncontrollable urgency. Ulcerative colitis is incurable. Living with this disease will be challenging, that is why I'm recommending surgery."

"What is the surgery, doctor?" Rachyl asked.

"We'll remove your damaged large intestine or colon and you will have to wear an ostomy bag. I know this seems extreme, but it's the only way for you to resume some normalcy to your life."

"No way, I'm not doing that. I don't care how many steroids I have to take, I'm never doing that."

"Okay, Rai, I understand this isn't an easy decision. We'll start with a steroid program and monitor your condition. Steroids are a temporary fix; if your condition worsens, surgery will be your only option."

After we left the doctor's office, I didn't leave my house for a year. The steroids would work for a while, but the pain would always come back. So, I ended up having the surgery. I started to develop terrible anxiety and depression. I would isolate myself and wonder, why did this happen to me? Why then? Was I making myself sick? Was I trying to find a way out? Was it stress? Was it fear? Whatever the reason, it was the worst thing that ever happened to me. So, I quit the band; that's when the music stopped, and my dream died.

♫   ♫   ♫

It's been fifteen years to the day, and I still think about it. I'm forty now, and I'm at that stage in life when you start to look back and reflect. What if I hadn't got sick? What if I hadn't met Rachyl? What if I hadn't quit? I miss playing music. It's weird, one day you wake up and realize you've become who you are. All your choices and all your hardships are just a distant memory and life just is.

I love my life now. I have two beautiful daughters and an amazing wife. I have a job that I enjoy, and great friends to hang out with. I have a new appreciation for my ostomy now. It took me some time, but I came to realize that it's better to have an ostomy and be able to live your life, then it is to live with the constant ups and downs of ulcerative colitis. But there's this little spark in me that still shines. When you have a passion for something, it's an obsession, it's hard to just stop. You can ignore it for a while, but eventually it creeps up on you. I miss my band. I miss the anticipation, the adrenaline, and the rush of the stage. I miss writing songs; it's my therapy.

It's early morning and the whole house is asleep. It's my favorite time of the day. This is my time to just sit and think. No noise, no commotion, just me, my coffee, and my thoughts. Of course, just as I sit at the breakfast table and pour milk on my cereal, my phone starts to vibrate. Maxx is calling.

"Hello."

"Hey, dummy."

My friends and I still talk to each other like we're back in high school. I've had the same group friends for twenty-five years now. They're vulgar, stubborn, and obnoxious. But, at the end of the day, we've been through a lot together, they're still my boys. Growing up in Toronto, you get to learn about all different cultures. The population is so diverse here, I've had friends of all different backgrounds and religions. Maxx is one of my closest buddies. We've made amends for ending the band. Once everyone knew how serious my illness was, they were incredibly supportive.

"What's up, pig. It's six in the morning, what the hell do you want?"

"Did you watch it last night?"

"Watch what?"

"*Remarkable,* obviously, you airhead."

"No, I couldn't. The girls were tired and Rachyl was working late. I had to lie in bed with them until they fell asleep. Why?"

"It was a crazy good episode, and at the end, they ran an ad for the upcoming season. They're looking for musicians. You should totally audition. You keep talking about how we could have made it, and how much you miss it; this is your chance, go for it!"

"I don't know, man. I'm old, bald, and chubby. I'm really not the rock star type anymore."

"That doesn't matter, man. You have the story and the talent, that's all they care about. All you have to do is sit in front of the camera and tell your story, while they get some actors to recreate it on screen. Come on, man, go for it!"

"Okay, calm down. I'll look into it. No promises."

"Alright, good; you still coming over to watch the hockey game tomorrow?"

"Yeah, I told Rachyl already. I'll be there."

"Cool, alright, later."

"Later."

Remarkable is this new reality show that everyone is talking about. Basically, they take everyday people who had to give up on their dreams an opportunity to showcase why they were remarkable. I doubt they'd pick me.

I shove a spoon full of cereal in my mouth, lean over to grab my laptop, flip it open, and search the show. The first thing that comes up is an article about a missing featured artist. I remember hearing about this story. Amy Strong went missing during her season of the show. The press has always assumed it was an overdose or suicide, and eventually the story faded away. Just another artist taken by the power of fame. The investigation is still ongoing. Before I can finish reading the article, I hear a little voice behind me.

"Hi, Daddy."

My little one, Alyssa, usually comes down right before I have to leave for work. I love it; I get to see her before I go. She's half asleep, wearing her purple onesie, and holding her stuffy under her arm.

"Good morning, Aly, how did you sleep?"

"Good. Daddy, I'm hungry."

"Okay, baby, come sit. I'll make you some cereal."

As I get up to make her a bowl, she slides onto my chair and starts eating my cereal. She strains her eyes as the bright light from the laptop is blinding this early in the morning.

"What are you doing, Daddy?" she asks, as she reaches for her glasses.

"Nothing, I was just reading something about music. Aly, can I ask you a question. Do you like Daddy's songs?"

"Of course, Dada, you're the best music player on the earth."

I slide her bowl of cereal in front of her and walk over to the laptop. I put on a few of my songs and smile as I watch her sing along.

"Okay, Aly, I have to go to work now. Stay here until Mom comes down. Kiss Nellie and Mommy for me. I'll see you tonight. Love you."

"Love you too, Daddy."

I give Aly a big hug and kiss on the forehead, grab my chef's roll, and make my way to work.

I know the restaurant is going to be busy today. I have so much "mise en place" to get through for a big function later tonight. Luckily, I scored the morning shift and will get to go home at a reasonable hour. Working in the food industry is a whole other world. We work long hours, are constantly on our feet, and working under immense pressure. When the whole world is enjoying their weekends and their holidays, we're hard at work making your family time special.

The day goes by surprisingly quick, considering all I can think about is that show. I've seen it a few times and I've always found it inspiring. To hear all the stories of pain and regret, only to be overcome, and replaced with gratitude and happiness in the end. I can relate to them. I deserve that chance, I just don't know if I'm good enough anymore. But, watching Alyssa sing my songs made me wonder if maybe I am? After what I've been through, I deserve this just as much as anyone.

As soon as I get home, I throw my keys on the counter, pull off my jacket, and head straight for the computer. I search the website and scroll down to their "contact us" section and find "submit your audition tape for 2020". I click on it, give them the gist of my story, upload a few songs, and hit send.

I feel a rare moment of inspiration to play my songs. I keep all my old gear at the ready in the basement, not that I go down there much. I'd love to say that I play guitar every day, but I'd be lying. As the years go on, the less I play, and the worse I feel I am at it. Every once in a while, I dust off the guitar, plug in the mic, and try to belt out a few of my old tunes.

I pick up my guitar, grab a pick from on top of the amplifier, and start strumming a few chords. I begin playing one of Rachyl's favorite songs. As soon as I start to sing, my voice starts to crack. My fingers slip off the fretboard, and the guitar lets out a dreadful rattle. It's a terrible feeling when you realize you've lost the skills to do something you love. I can't do it anymore. Who am I kidding? I can't do this. I switch everything off, place my guitar back on the stand, and make my way upstairs.

I walk into the kitchen and see Rachyl. She's wearing her favorite fuzzy grey sweater, skinny jeans, and has her turquoise glasses on. She's got some old nineties rock tunes playing and she's doing her best to sing along. I still get butterflies when she enters a room. She has the most beautiful green eyes you've ever seen.

She walks over to the stove and opens the oven. Our family is on a vegetarian kick right now. At first, I wasn't a big fan, but I prefer it now. She's a great cook. When we first met her diet consisted of Kraft Dinner and Mr. Noodles. I helped with her cooking skills along the way, but she'll never admit it. Even though I'm a chef, she does most of the cooking.

"Hey, when did you get home? I didn't hear you come in."

"Not too long ago. I went downstairs to play a little guitar. How was your day?"

"That's nice; I love when you play your old songs. My day wasn't bad, work was crazy, and then the kids were driving me nuts. Pretty normal day."

"Hey, I wanted to ask you something; that show, *Remarkable*, what do you think about me auditioning?"

"I didn't want to say anything, but I was hoping you'd do it."

"Really? You think they'd pick me? You're the second person to tell me that. Maxx was telling me to audition."

"Well, are you?" she asks.

"Maybe. I'll think about it. I'm not sure I still got "it"."

"Of course you still got it, you never lost it. I'm not going to pressure you, just do what makes you happy. Either way, I'll support you. But promise me, you won't do anything before telling me and the girls first."

"I won't, I promise. What's for dinner?"

"I made veggie quesadillas and I picked up some ice cream for dessert."

"Let me guess, pistachio?"

"Yes, you know it's my favorite. Don't worry, I got a different one for you guys. Can you call the kids, please, dinner is ready."

"Guys! Dinner!"

I don't want to tell Rachyl I submitted my songs and story yet. There's no way they're going to pick me anyway, and the rejection will be much easier to handle if no one else knows. My insecurities always take over in these moments.

The kids come running into the kitchen and jump into their spots. Rachyl brings the food over and places it in the middle of the table. We all sit, laugh, tell stories about our day, and enjoy our family dinner together.

CHAPTER TWO

It's been a few weeks and I haven't heard anything from *Remarkable*. The kids are in school, Rachyl is at work, and I have the day off. All this music talk is giving me the itch to play. I head downstairs and start up the equipment again.

I start with a few old songs and it feels good this time. My vocals are actually sounding decent and I get through the songs without missing a note; maybe I do still got it. I mess around with a few chords and try and write a new tune. It's been awhile since I wrote a new song. Sometimes I think musicians have a song writing expiration date. Writing songs early on felt so effortless and the songs all came out sounding like hits. When you're at the peak of your songwriting, songs seem to come out of thin air, but now it feels like I'm reaching for something that just isn't there. I try and hear the melody, but nothing is coming to me. I get through a few versus, scribble down some lyrics, and switch everything off.

I make my way upstairs, load up the coffee machine, and check my emails. There's a message from the show. It says I've been selected to the next phase of the audition. I'm to come to their downtown office today and meet with a guide. Even though I'm reading it, I still don't believe it. I'm sure a bunch of people got the same message. I sip my coffee and try and make sense of what to do.

Turing forty is a strange time in anyone's life. It's like a chemical in your mind releases these new thoughts and feelings. A few months ago, I would have never even considered doing something like this. But something inside me is telling me to go for it. I owe it to myself to take this opportunity, after my chance slipped away all those years ago. I think about my daughter singing along to my songs, and how Rachyl fell in love with me because of music. Besides, the message only says next phase, so I haven't even been chosen yet. If anything, it will be an experience, even if they don't end up picking me. I'm going for it.

It's early February in Toronto and I haven't seen a blue sky in weeks. It's always chilly and overcast this time of year. The snow is melting but it's still slushy, and my car is forever dirty from all the salt trucks. Traveling downtown is always a struggle for me. We live about an hour away and the traffic is always terrible. I'm traumatized from having colitis all those years; I'm always making sure I know where the nearest bathrooms are. But I make it there just in time.

The *Remarkable* building is located in Yorkville, a fashionable part of downtown where all the new chic companies are found. As I get closer, I can see a second building connected to it. I follow the signs and enter the head office building.

The office space is small, but comfortable. There's a receptionist at the front desk. I walk up nervously and wait as he finishes with his phone call.

"Hi, I got an email from you guys to come in."

"Great, your name?" he asks.

"Rai Starings."

"Okay, Rai, have a seat and your guide will be with you shortly."

"Thank you."

I walk over to the empty lounge and sit in the nearest chair. The glass coffee table is stocked with celebrity magazines spread neatly down the middle. I notice three abstract paintings of elephants on the wall and a giant fern tucked in the far corner.

"Right this way, Mr. Starings."

I follow the receptionist down a narrow hallway to a room that looks like a combination of a doctor's office and science lab. There are computers, medical equipment, and strange machines everywhere. Before the door can close behind me, a man walks in from a door at the other end of the room.

"Hello, my name is Henry. I'll be your guide."

He adjusts his thick black reading glasses and spins into his office chair.

"So, Starr, tell me, why are you here?"

It takes me a second to realize that he just called me Starr.

"A couple of people close to me told me I should audition for the show. I was in a rock band back in the day, but I had to stop. Sometimes I think about my life and how I wish I could go back and do things differently. I hear you do that here, so here I am. Wait, sorry, did you just call me Starr?"

"That's what you prefer to be called, isn't it?"

"Well, most of my friends call me Starr because of my last name; it was my stage name, but how do you know that?"

"We do our research here. Let's see, fifteen years ago you were in a band called Divine Light, correct?"

"Yes."

"Now you're a chef, you have a wife, two kids, and I'm sorry to hear about your father's passing, my condolences."

"Wow, you really do your research. You seem to know a lot about me, but I don't know much about you. What exactly do you do here?"

"Well, simply put, I'm a guide for those lucky enough to relive a moment in their life. Here at *Remarkable*, we give people like yourself the opportunity to go back to a point in their life where they walked away from their dreams, and we let them relive it."

"Are you saying I'm one of those lucky people?"

"I am indeed. You have a special story and extraordinary music, the world needs to hear it. Only one individual each year is featured in our program; we've chosen you."

"Really? Why me?"

"The moment we heard your music, we knew. There's something unique about your sound. As we dug deeper, we learned about your unfortunate disability, and we felt you deserved a second chance."

I think to myself, this seems almost too good to be true. I have so many questions, but I must admit, it feels good to hear my music appreciated.

"How exactly do you do this? Is there a set and a script? I'm not an actor. How does it all work?" I ask.

"Not exactly. This room is a program chamber, this is where you will enter the program. First, your mind will be connected to our computers using a neural headset. Then, we will sedate you, placing you in a deep sleep. We'll inject a serum in your bloodstream containing special molecules that will allow our program to travel through your memories. We will locate the exact moment where you strayed from your dreams and awaken your subconscious in the program. Everything you do from that point on will be relived in your mind, and we press record. We will help generate the backdrop, but the outcome and the storyline will be up to you."

"Wait. So, there are no actors? It all happens in a computer program in my head?"

"Exactly, all the people in your life will exist in the program as they did fifteen years ago, as will you. A virtual world is much more cost efficient then creating a real one. We alter everyone's appearance just enough to make it seem like a production, and to avoid any unwanted lawsuits. You'll only be here for a few nights, three or four sessions at the most, once a week. We don't recommend more than that. Time ticks differently in the program. We will have all the film we need. It will take us a few days to edit it, and a few days to promote it. Then, the episodes will air, and you will be the next star of *Remarkable*."

"That's crazy, it looks so real. I always thought it was actors. Why haven't I heard about this? And what's in this serum?"

"Some people have a moral problem with creating a virtual world. To avoid any troubles, we prefer to keep this information on a need to know basis. But I can assure you, everything is safe, tested, and certified by the Federal Communications Commission. While you're asleep, your body will be monitored by a medical professional. The memory serum is complex. Amongst other things, it contains copious amounts of elephant neurons, due to their excellent memories."

I take a second to think about it. I know I should talk to Rachyl first. I don't usually make snap decisions like this. I'm always over-analyzing everything, trying to find something wrong with it. This sounds crazy, but you know what, this is my chance to make things right. A second chance to do what I've always dreamed of doing. Plus, Rachyl told me I should do it. I deserve this. Before I can answer, Henry says,

"I must make something perfectly clear. If you do this, you will lose the lifestyle that you and your family are accustomed to. Privacy and freedom are things we all take for granted. Fame can take its toll on a person, it's dangerous. You will transform from being someone with little means, to being an instant celebrity. But one thing I can assure you, all those regrets you've been carrying around about not following your musical dreams will be gone. If you accept, you will start right now. I have all the paperwork ready for you to sign. Is this something you're willing to accept?"

Almost uncontrollably, my heart answers before my mind can process the risks. "I'm in. Where do I sign?"

I sign all the appropriate paperwork and Henry shows me where to get undressed. He hands me a hospital gown and a plastic bag for all my belongings. My mind is racing, and my body is sweating, I can't believe I'm doing this. My whole life I've put others before myself, it's in my nature, but this time I know, I need to do this, for me.

I walk back into the chamber room and lie flat on the chair. Henry begins to hook me up to the machine. I feel a cold, mesh-like metal material covering the top of my head. Small wires gently crawl down the side of my head and attach to my temples. Henry hangs a saline bag on an IV pole and inserts a needle in my left arm where the fluids will enter. Then, he fills a syringe with a fluorescent purple serum and places it on the tray beside him. He grabs the gas mask and begins to administer the sedation. I start to think about what Henry said, about my freedom, about my family. Regret starts to set in. The room suddenly becomes cold and the hum of the machine becomes louder.

"Starr. Can you hear me?" Henry asks.

"Yes."

Two figures walk in through a door on the opposite side of the chamber. It's hard for me to make out who they are, as the sedation begins to take over. Henry comes in close and tells me something that only he and I can hear.

"Rai. When you're in the program, if you ever feel lost or helpless, call for me."

"How?" I ask.

"Just call out my name, I'll be watching." Henry backs up quickly and continues with his directions. "Okay, Starr, close your eyes and count back from thirty."

I begin to count down. Thirty... I can't believe I'm doing this. Twenty-nine... Am I that crazy to trust this guy? Twenty-eight... Do I want this so badly that I would give up my whole life? Twenty-seven... I can't do it, get me out of here. Twenty-six...

"Starr. Starr. Starr!" Rikki yells from behind the drum kit as I look back at him from behind the microphone. "Snap out of it!"

It's too late. I'm in...

CHAPTER THREE

Higgins and Rikki start playing our opening song like we always did. Somehow, I remember the words like it was yesterday. We're playing The Reverb on Queen Street, I'm sure of it. The stage is just as I remember. The familiar heat of the spotlight hits my face, and the smell brings me right back to where I belong. I can feel the buzz in the air. I'm back. I can't believe it.

Maxx is playing bass. I can't remember when he started playing with us. We went through a bunch of bassists that never really worked out. I always wanted Maxx to play the bass, but he wasn't into music like I was. I bought him a cheap amp and a bass, hoping he would come around, finally I convinced him. He's not the best bassist in the world, but he's a character, and a good piece to the puzzle. He's always over-dressed, but that's his style.

Rikki Stixx is a hard pounding, hit you in the chest kind of drummer. He has crazy long hair and is built like a truck. If you met him on the street, you'd never think he was a drummer. He looks more like someone you'd find on a construction site.

Higgins, on the other hand, is undoubtedly a lead guitarist. He's always wearing a black leather jacket, tight jeans, and a feathered fedora on his head. He's bone-thin with hair long enough to just cover his eyes. The four of us make for an odd group of misfits. Our sound is definitely 90s alternative rock. Some say we're a cross between the old Weezer albums and Nirvana.

We're almost done our thirty-minute set, but I never want it to end. I play with my eyes closed and feel the music flowing out of me. My voice has never been the greatest but our melody and harmonies more than make up for it. I open my eyes and address the crowd before we play our closer.

"Hey guys, listen. I just wanted to say how lucky we are to be playing in front of you right now. It truly is a dream come true. This last one is called, *I'll try to feel alive.*"

It's funny how I wrote this song so long ago, yet the title fits so perfectly. I love this song, which is rare for me. Usually, I only like my songs when I first write them, then about a week later I'm sick of them. I remember writing this one. It's about knowing when something is about to end, and desperately trying to save it.

As we start our build up, I feel my heart racing and my mind gets lost. It's as close to a high as you can get without the help of hard narcotics. Playing live is an out of body experience. I come to earth just in time to say a few words to close the show.

"That's it, thank you, Toronto. We are Divine Light. You guys are amazing."

This is where we usually bust out an oldie just to catch the crowd off guard. I remember this night, we ended with the guitar solo portion of Pink Floyd's *Comfortably Numb*. Higgins hasn't missed a beat. His guitar solo is bang on and Rikki is hitting the kick drum so hard I can feel it in my chest. I remember this gig because it was a big one; it's when I met Rachyl.

After our set, the boys and I head backstage for some drinks. This is our time to talk about the show and hang out a little before we catch the rest of the acts.

"Eh, what happened to you at the start? I almost told Maxx to go give you a slap and snap you out of it," Rikki says.

"Yeah, sorry boys. I forgot where I was for a second there, my bad."

"Starr, beer me." I throw Higgins a cold one, just as Maxx asks me,

"Did you bring the weed?"

I forgot, I was smoking pot back then and I was the one who always scored the grass. I instinctively reach into my pocket and feel a little baggie inside. It's been awhile since I last smoked; this should be interesting. Without thinking about it, I take two hits and it floors me. Wait, I wasn't supposed to smoke up tonight. I remember Rachyl saying she would never be with anyone who did drugs, that's why I quit. Hopefully, our meeting before the show and the kiss in the parking lot was enough. Of course, as soon as I realize this, the door swings open and I see Dawn, Higgins' girlfriend and one of Rachyl's best friends. She knows about her no drug policy. She sees me, lit joint in my hands and looking guilty as hell; I'm screwed.

"Wow, it smells like a skunk died in here. Great show, guys! Hey, Rai."

"Hey, Dawn. Listen, please don't tell Rachyl about this. It's my last one, I swear."

"Don't worry, I won't."

I know that's a lie. She's going to tell her as soon as she sees her. I'm such an idiot. I can't believe I did this. What am I going to do? I make my way to the bathroom to try and sober up. On the way, I see June coming straight for me. June is another one of Rachyl's best friends, she's more like a sister than anything. She's tall, beautiful, and very smart. Smart enough to know when someone's under the influence.

"Rai, you guys were so good tonight!"

"Thanks, June, thanks for coming. Where's Rachyl?"

"She's at the bar with Dawn and Higgins; are you coming?"

"Yeah, sure, I'll be right there, I just gotta use the bathroom first." I slip away.

As I stare at myself in this grimy downtown bathroom mirror, I can see that I'm a mess. I look like a junkie. I can't go talk to her like this. I have to get out of here. Where do I go? I know, the one place me and my idiot friends always went to hang out, The Unit. I grab my gear and head straight out the back door. I jump into a cab and tell the driver the address,

"Hey man, nineteen Edgely Street please, and quick."

When I was eighteen, I had the bright idea to rent out a small unit over a winter jacket store in a strip mall plaza. Instead of opening a business, we made it a place to hang out. We picked the most secluded place we could find and made sure that all the businesses around were closed in the evenings and weekends. It cost us fifty dollars each, a small price to pay for teenage freedom. It was fun, but it got ugly fast. Picture six eighteen-year-old boys with no responsibility living together with no one around.

As I walk in, the unit looks exactly as I remember it. There are empty pizza boxes stacked to the ceiling and Molson Canadian beer bottles nesting hundreds of fruit flies. The place wreaks of fast food, smoke, and stale beer. We tried our best to make it as comfortable as we could. We built our own bar out of cinder blocks, installed a bunch of nice lights, and bought a kick ass entertainment center. There's a big beige hand me down couch, like the one that would sit in your aunt's basement, and an old recliner. There's one bedroom, a bathroom with a shower, and a pretty cool jam room to play our music.

As usual, some of the guys are here playing cards. These are the friends that are either too cheap to go out, or are severely antisocial, probably due to years of smoking pot. But, after the day I'm having, I'm happy they're here to keep me company. I can't believe how young everyone looks.

"What's up, fat heads?" I say, trying to act as normal as possible.

"What's up, loser, you're back early. What happened? Did you get booed off the stage again?"

"Nah, we went on early and I didn't feel like sticking around, so I jet."

"Where's the rest of the bums?"

"They're all going to an after party; I wasn't feeling it tonight. I just wanna chill."

"Alright, we're about to deal another game of Texas hold 'em, you want in?"

"Nah, I gotta put all my gear away, maybe later."

I head straight to the jam room to figure out what I'm going to do. I take a second to breathe. I sit on the dirty floor, next to my Marshall guitar amp, and think.

"Okay, It's fine. I'm back with the band, and Rachyl is here. I screwed up tonight, but I can still do this. It's just a dream. All I have to do, is do what I've always wanted to do, play music. Once all this is over, I'll go back to my family, and everything will be back to normal."

I quickly realize there's nothing normal about this. I try to convince myself that everything is fine, but I'm freaking out inside. I look down and rub my hand down the right side of my stomach; my ostomy is gone. I stare at my reflection through the gloss of my guitar and notice I look younger and different. This is crazy; Henry said to call for him if I ever needed help. I know I just got here, but I'm freaking out.

"Henry?" As soon as his name comes out of my mouth, I hear the guys calling for me.

"Starr, some dude is at the door for you; he wants you to go outside. He said he met you at the show."

I sprint down the stairs and look outside. Someone is standing there, but it's not Henry. At least, it doesn't look like Henry.

"Can I help you?" I ask.

"Starr, it's me, Henry."

"Henry?"

"Quick, act normal so we don't draw attention to ourselves. I'll explain in the car. Get in, let's go."

Henry walks over to the passenger side door of his car and opens it. I recognize the car. It's a 2005 Honda Insight, one of the first hybrid-electric cars. It looks like a regular car on the outside, but the inside is no ordinary car. There are buttons and screens everywhere. This has to be Henry.

"Hey man, I'm sorry I called you so quickly, but you said if I ever needed..." Henry holds up his hand, gesturing for me to stop talking. We pull into a small garage tucked under the highway underpass. Henry pushes a button directly over his head and the door quickly closes behind us.

"Okay, we're safe, we can talk now. Are you alright?"

"I'm fine, I'm not in trouble or anything, I'm just freaking out. I saw Rachyl and I screwed up bad. I totally forgot she was going to be at that show, and I smoked up. She hates that, she's going to kill me."

"You don't have to worry about Rachyl, that's the least of your worries. You love each other. She'll be there, waiting for you when this is all over. Remember, this is not about you and Rachyl, this is about you, doing what you love."

"What do I have to worry about then?" I ask.

"There is something you should know. The people that own this show, they don't care about you or your family. To them, it's all about business. All they care about are money and ratings. I'm a programmer. I created this world. The program that *Remarkable* uses is my masterpiece. There have been problems in the past with a previous artist."

"I read about this, Amy, right? What happened to her?"

"No one knows. But I don't want anything like that to happen again. So, I created a wormhole to access the program. I use this car to travel in and out and make sure you guys are safe, so don't worry. Rai, this is your chance to relive your dreams. Don't let anything get in your way. I created this program to help people find peace in their life. This is your time, use it, make it count."

"Thanks, Henry, I needed this talk. Sorry I freaked out, it's just so real, it's amazing, I can't believe this is happening. I have so many questions."

"Don't worry, I get it. It's a lot to take in on the first session. What do you want to know?"

"What happens if I get hurt or worse?"

"Small injuries will not affect you differently in the program, you'll feel the same pain as you would in the real world. Death however is problematic. Your virtual self would die in the program, but your body in the chamber would not. You would go into neurogenic shock; it won't be fun, but can be treated in most cases. The same would happen if you were pulled from the program prematurely. Your body can't take the shock, the serum needs to run its course."

"And how do I get out?" I ask.

"The serum has different dosages, the higher the dosage, the longer you have in the program. Once the serum has gone through your system, you will slowly wake up from your dream, just like you do every morning."

"I have so many more questions, but I can't think of anything right now. This is all just so crazy."

"I know, just try and enjoy it. This is it, this is what you've always wanted."

After speaking with Henry, I begin to feel more at ease. As we speed back to the unit, I'm actually excited to get back in that jam room and start writing again. The melodies and riffs are already flowing in my head, I can feel it. I open the car door and jump out. Before Henry leaves, he rolls down his window and says,

"Rai, you have a second chance to do what you love. Not many people get this opportunity. Think back to the way you felt when you were doing what you loved to do. It's all about the music. Try not to worry too much, I'll be watching. Be safe, peace."

"Thanks, Henry."

I open the unit door and run up the dirty stairs. The guys start ragging on me, but I can't hear them. All I can hear are the melodies in my head. I miss writing music so much. It's such an amazing feeling to just get lost in a song. I was devastated when I couldn't do it anymore. It was like a part of me died. Songwriting is difficult to describe, everyone has their own process. Sometimes writing great music is something that just happens. It comes to you and flows out of you; it's magical. It's not something you can force or plan for. The best thing to do is give the magic a reason to happen and have the tools to bring it to life. That's why most songs are about heartbreak or troubled times. The artist didn't plan for those bad things to happen, they just did, and the result was an incredible song. The more risks you take in life, the more opportunity you create for that magic to happen. This morning I couldn't write a song, but now, because I took this incredible risk, the magic is back.

I head straight for the jam room and open my guitar case. My old acoustic guitar, my Taylor, is staring back at me. I loved this guitar. I loathed the day I had to sell it. Times were tough, and Rachyl and I had to find money somewhere to pay the mortgage, so I sold it. I lift it from its case and rest it on my lap. I take a second to feel it and smell it. Some guitars are hard to play, but this feels soft and smooth. It almost feels like it's playing itself.

My song writing always starts with a riff. I play a few chords and hum a few melodies until it clicks. I must have been in there for hours playing the same song. I lose track of time when I'm really writing. I know it's time to stop when my fingers start getting tired. Lyrics are always secondary for me. They're usually scribbles on a bunch of scrap paper at first, until I find the right words. The way the words sound is more important to me than the actual words. I hate lyrics that are too direct or literal. People often ask me what my songs are about. I always say, "What do they mean to you?" I want people to feel what I was feeling, rather than know what I was thinking. Great songs help you when you're going through tough times. We all have different obstacles in life, and it's amazing when a song can make so many different people feel like it was written just for them. That's what makes it magical.

Someone bangs on the jam room door and shouts,

"Starr? Are you in there?"

"Yeah, what's up Maxx?"

"It's ten in the morning, man. Don't you have work today? What happened to you last night? That Rachyl girl was pissed, man."

I come out of the jam room looking like a zombie. Maxx looks at me like I'm a mad man. I put my hand on his shoulder.

"Sorry, man. I had this song in my head and had to get it out."

"Sick, let's hear it."

We go back in the jam room and I start playing. He stops me after a few seconds and grabs his bass. These are the moments I miss, just me and Maxx playing music together. Nothing else in the world matters but this song. After a few minutes, he stops.

"I don't think you're going to work today. You did it man, this is the one. This is the song that's going to make it. I can't believe you wrote this. How did you do it?"

"I don't know, I came in here, picked up my guitar and it just happened."

"Well, get ready, buddy. We have our hit."

CHAPTER FOUR

Later that night I call for a band practice. Maxx is already here when Rikki and Higgins arrive. The beers start flowing, and the weed is burning. The guys are stoked about the new songs that Maxx and I are rehearsing. Everyone adds their little touches that really make the songs come together. As a chef, I think of music like food; it's an art. Like a great dish, a little salt here, a little lemon juice there, can turn a good dish into an exceptional one. A great song is no different. It needs a little harmony here, a little drum fill there, to become a classic.

We play for hours and have never sounded better. I often think about all the iconic songs like, *Bohemian Rhapsody, Imagine,* and *Smells Like Teen Spirit,* and wonder how they were written. Someone sat down and wrote those songs, walked into a rehearsal, and said, "Hey, guys, what do you think about this?" and played a masterpiece. Imagine being in the room when Jimmy Page and Robert Plant were writing *Stairway to Heaven.* It seems impossible, but it happens. Unfortunately, as songwriters know, this gift doesn't last forever. The lucky ones can write two or three, but eventually we all lose the magic.

For the next two weeks in the program we're locked away in the jam room writing and rehearsing songs. Higgins and Rikki are working their asses off promoting and lining up gigs. Every show we play gets bigger and better. The crowds are really responding to the new tunes. You can feel the music buzz in the air, and we're a big part of it. We also begin noticing people in suits coming to our shows, which can only mean one thing, agents.

We play about six shows before it happens. It's our biggest gig to date. We're opening for Sloan, a great Canadian band, at the historic Opera House in downtown Toronto. We're breaking down our equipment when we hear a voice; we turn around and see someone standing just off stage. She's about thirty, wearing a black 'Broken Social Scene' T-shirt, skinny jeans, and an oversized wool cardigan. She has short black hair, a nose ring, and spacers in her earlobes. She's the definition of a rock chick.

"Hey, guys, you sounded amazing tonight. My name's Dani. I own SubRock Records. I really liked what I heard tonight. That song, *Five Long Years*, is an instant classic. I had goosebumps. Let me buy you guys a drink."

Dani slips me her business card and walks us to the bar. After about three drinks and a few laughs she hits us with it.

"Listen, guys, I've been to a lot of shows recently and I've seen plenty of good bands. At SubRock, we aren't interested in good bands, we want great bands. Your songs are amazing. I felt the years of pain and heartache in your songs, and from such a young band, it's remarkable. The first time I saw you guys, I was blown away. But I wanted to see a few more shows before I approached you. Every show was better and better; I'm a big fan."

"Thanks, Dani, we've been waiting to hear those words for a long time. Tell us a bit about SubRock, I haven't heard of them," I say, even though inside I'm reaching for my pen and dying to sign the papers.

"Sure. We're a young independent company starting to fill our roster. We're very selective about the artists we want to work with. We have a few small acts signed, but you guys are what we've been waiting for. We do things a little differently at SubRock. You'll have total creative control, and we'll work together to find cool ways to promote and get your music out there. We can't give you any money up front, but I know once we get started it won't take long for you guys to start making a decent living."

This is the type of record company I've always wanted to work with, small, artistic, creative, and innovative. Just then, a tall, older gentleman wearing a black suit and tie, interrupts our conversation.

"Hey guys, great show. I'm Doug, from Reckless Records."

We've all heard of Reckless Records. They've signed all the biggest stars. Their list of clients is the who's who of the music industry. The rest of the guys in the band are star struck and switch their attention to Doug, as Dani and I step back. She looks defeated. She grabs my arm and says,

"That guy has been following me for weeks. Every time I talk to a band, he swoops in and flashes his card. Just like the rest of the world, the rich get richer. Well, I guess that's that. He is going to sign you guys. Good luck, you're gonna need it."

"Hold on, the last thing I want to do is come this far and sell out to some bigwig recording company. Trust me, we want to sign with SubRock."

"Is that so, is that why your guys are signing those papers right now? Look behind you."

I turn my head and see Maxx, Rikki, and Higgins smiling and laughing. Maxx has a pen in his hand and is signing on the dotted line. He waves me over. I turn back to Dani.

"Don't worry, I'll be right back. Don't leave."

I run over to Maxx and grab the pen, but it's too late, the papers are signed. I look back to find Dani, but she's gone, lost in the crowd.

"You must be Rai Starr. Congratulations, you're going to be signed to a major label. Divine Night is going to be huge!"

"It's Divine Light, our band is called Divine Light."

"Divine Light, right, right. You guys are going to be massive."

Doug pats me on the back, gathers his paperwork and leaves. I take a second to calm my nerves before I totally lose my cool. I'm pissed, but the rest of the guys are elated. They're all hugging and high fiving each other like they just won the lottery.

"Guys, what the hell? You just blew off Dani."

"Forget about SubRock, they're nobodies," says Maxx. "This is Reckless Records, man, this is the big time. We did it!"

He tries to hug me, but I want nothing of it. I come back with fire in my eyes, directing my rage at all of them.

"Do you really think he cares about us? Dani, she cared, man. She knew our songs and she came to all our shows. This dummy didn't even know our name."

"What's your problem, man? Chill out, it's just a letter of intent, we haven't signed officially yet. Besides, this isn't just your decision, we all have to decide. We talked about it and this is what we want to do. We get a fat bonus if we sign. She wasn't giving us squat," Maxx says.

"So that's it then, Maxx, money? That's what you guys care about? Did you even read the papers? What about creative control, distribution, royalties? Did he even mention any of those things? And what about my vote?"

Maxx is quiet for a change. He turns his back on me and walks towards the other guys.

"Rai, don't worry," says Higgins. "You'll have a chance to look at all the details when it comes time to officially sign. The vote is three to one, dude. You were too busy talking with that Dani girl.

Listen man, we're brothers, let's embrace this. We honestly thought you of all people would be happy."

"Well, I'm not. But if this what the band wants, fine. You guys better be right about this."

♫　　♫　　♫

"Sam, can you come into my office please."

Jack leans back in his red velvet chair. He sips from his oversized wine glass and admires his new veneers in his desk mirror.

"Coming, my love." His wife hurries in, her laptop tucked under her arm.

"Do we have any other appointments today?"

"Nothing worth pursuing. So, how do you feel about Rai Starr? Amazing right?"

"I saw a few minutes of tape. I love his story. I think people will really relate to him. Let's see how he does. What do the numbers look like this month?"

"I think we're going to have our best month this year. I spoke with two more stations today that want to air us."

"I told you this would work. What did you tell them?"

"I told them *Remarkable* will be the number-one-rated reality show on television by the end of the quarter, and the going rate is two million an episode."

"Wonderful. Let's be careful now. We're getting big. The FCC wants us to lie low, people are starting to ask questions. Where's Henry?"

"He's in the chamber, working with Rai. Henry thinks he's special, but he's worried it might happen again."

"Tell Henry to relax, nothing is going to happen," says Jack. "As long as Rai sticks to the music, all will be alright in the end. I'm more worried about the FCC shutting us down. Make sure we keep the money flowing their way. Do we have the rights to Rai's music?"

"Henry said Rai signed all the papers without hesitation. Once the public watches the show and hears his music, we'll have the number one show and the number one album in the world."

Jack and Sam Cranney are the founders of one of the biggest entertainment companies in the world, the creators of the reality show *Remarkable*, and a thriving recording company called Reckless Records. They first met in medical school. Sam has a degree in Psychology and Jack a Bachelor of Science. Though their education was impressive, they always dreamed of developing something more extraordinary together. So, they started a small production company which grew to become the giant corporation it is today. As powerful and popular as they are, they are equally as private. Rarely are they seen in public and their studio is connected to their million-dollar loft.

Sam walks over to the office bar and selects a cappuccino from the imported Italian coffee machine. Jack brings his wine and sits at one of the bar stools.

"Sam, you're a genius; how did you know Rai would take the drugs?"

"I knew if Rachyl was in the picture, he'd lose focus. So, I made sure Henry programmed the weed in his pocket, then I knew the excitement of the moment would be enough for him to forget about her no drug policy. It was the easiest way to get rid of her."

"Do you think Dawn is going to tell Rachyl?"

Sam walks over to Jack and sits on his lap. She kisses his neck softly and runs her fingers through his hair.

"She already did, and so did June. It's over. It's all about the music now."

"What about Amy, what are we going to do with her?" Jack asks.

"I'm not sure. Let's leave her in the program for now."

CHAPTER FIVE

As I open my eyes, the bright fluorescent strip lights are blinding. I finally come to as the serum wears off. A cool breeze from the rattling air conditioning unit gently flows up my hospital gown. Soft beeps echo from the machine beside me, as the feeling begins to come back to my arms. I can feel the itch from under the intravenous every time I shift positions. I look down and see my ostomy; I'm back in the real world now. What seemed like weeks in the program was only a few hours of deep sleep. I've been in this chamber all night; Rachyl is going to kill me.

"Morning, sunshine, how are you feeling?" Henry asks, as he walks in to check up on me.

"A little woozy, but I'm okay."

"Don't worry, that's normal, your body needs time to adapt to the effects of the serum. It will become much easier to recover the more your body is exposed. So, what did you think of the program?"

"It felt so real. I was a little nervous in the beginning, but once I settled in, it was like I was twenty-five again. The sounds, the smells, the people, it was so genuine. I can't believe it."

Henry begins to unhook me from the program. With a few clicks on the computer screen, the small wires gently detach from my temples, and slowly retract into the headset. Henry pulls the IV from my arm and tapes a small piece of gauze over the injection spot. I want to talk about our meet-up in the program, but I'm getting a sense that I shouldn't.

"Okay, Rai, we're all done for today. Your clothes and belongings are in the bag beside you. Take your time, I'll be in the hall when you're done." Henry turns to leave the chamber.

"Henry, wait. I just wanted to say, I never thought I would ever get the chance to play my music again. Thank you."

"You're welcome. Just remember, it's easy to get lost in that world. You're here to relive your dream, then get back to what's most important - your family."

As Henry is talking, I can hear my phone buzzing. I search through my bag and find my phone. I see six missed calls, ten unread texts, and two voicemails. All from Rachyl. Henry leaves the chamber and I call her as fast as I can.

"Rai! Where are you? Are you okay? I've been worried sick!"

"Oh my God, I'm so sorry. I fell asleep at Maxx's. I told you I was going, remember? We were watching the hockey game and I dozed off. I'm such an idiot. I'm so sorry."

"Don't scare me like that. You know I don't like it when I can't reach you. What if something happened to me or the kids?"

"I know, I know, I'm sorry. I'm leaving right now."

"I'm glad you're alright, don't do that again! Hurry home, bye."

"Love you, bye."

I quickly call Maxx. He's not answering. I wait and leave a message.

"Hey, man, I'm sorry about ditching last night. Listen, I did something crazy and I need a favor. I told Rachyl that I crashed at your house last night. Can you cover for me in case she calls? I'll explain later, call me back." I hang up and finish getting dressed.

I rush to find Henry so I can get home to Rachyl before she really gets mad. I walk out the door into the hall. Henry is standing against the wall waiting for me.

"Henry, I have to go. I just got off the phone with Rachyl; she is not happy."

"Listen, Rai, Jack Cranney wants to talk to you. He's the owner. He likes to have a one-on-one with the artists before the show goes live. It will only take a minute; are you okay with that?"

I pause before I answer. I know Henry said these are bad people. But I need to see for myself.

"Okay, but I can't stay for long."

Henry leads me down the bright white hallway that ends with a set of elevators. The elevator doors open, and we walk in. Henry swipes his ID card and pushes the penthouse button. Before the doors open, I whisper to Henry,

"Henry, about what we talked about…"

Henry uses his eyes to direct my attention to the elevator camera and microphone.

"Everything is fine, Rai, just talk to Jack. You'll find out all you need to know."

Henry holds the elevator door open for me and points me in the right direction. He stares at me intensely as he pushes the button and the doors begin to close.

The penthouse is huge; this must be the mansion connected to the building. The hardwood floor is gleaming, and countless white plush rugs are tucked neatly under every piece of furniture. The wallpaper has a modern design, and the crystal chandeliers are emitting just the right amount of light. A scent of citrus fills the air, as a stream of smoke rises from the oval-shaped essential oil diffuser. The windows are tinted in such a way that you can see out, but not in.

"Rai, Rai Starr, is that you?" Jack reaches for my hand. "I'm Jack. I'm looking forward to getting to know you."

"Likewise. Nice to meet you."

"So, Henry tells me you enjoyed your first session. Come, have a seat. Can I offer you a drink?"

"No, thank you, I can't stay long. Yes, what an amazing experience. I still can't believe it. It feels so real."

"That's because it is real, in a sense. It's your memories, and your experiences. We just set the stage and the rest is up to you. Henry is a gifted programmer, isn't he?"

"He really is. His program is truly a life-changing invention. I'm just worried I'm not doing it justice. Listen, Mr. Cranney."

"Please, call me Jack."

"Sorry, Jack. I'm not sure what I'm supposed to do or why you chose me. This is all happening so fast. I want to make sure I'm doing everything right and I'm not letting anybody down. I know this show is important and people love it. I don't want to mess it up for everybody."

"You're doing great, Rai. Just do what you feel is right when you're in the program. You wanted to be a rock star, this is your chance to be one. Just remember everyone is watching, and they want to be entertained. At the end of the day, we want *Remarkable* to be the biggest show on television and for you to be the next superstar. We chose you because we know you have it in you. Be reckless, take risks and be daring, that's what people want to see."

Jack takes a sip of his shiraz and leans back in his leather chair. Just then a woman enters the room.

"You must be Rai Star, I'm Sam, Jack's wife. Great to finally meet you."

"Nice to meet you too. Thank you for inviting me, lovely home you guys have here."

"Thank you, we like it. It's private, cozy, and, as you can tell, close to work. Tell me, how are you dealing with being in the program? I can image it's overwhelming."

But before I can answer, Jack says, "Sam has a degree in Psychology. She's in charge of your mental state. I'm in medicine myself, I take care of your physical wellbeing. We just want to make sure you can handle all of this. Fame is a powerful thing, Rai."

"I'm more worried about what to tell my wife, to be honest. I haven't told her yet. It is a lot, but exciting at the same time. This is what I've always wanted to do. I've lived with regret for so long, I finally feel alive again. I just want everything to go well."

"That's great to hear, Rai," says Sam. "We don't want to keep your wife waiting. You're free to go. Just remember, if you need anything, please ask. We'll do our best to help."

"Thank you, Sam, I will. Before I leave, I do have one question. Henry mentioned there was a problem with a previous artist. What happened exactly?"

Jack and Sam look at each other, then look down. It takes a moment before Jack answers.

"Nobody is exactly sure, Rai. We all have our struggles in life. Fame seems amazing from afar, but you never really know how someone is feeling inside. That's why it's important to talk to Sam when times get tough. Amy was troubled, that's all we know."

"Well, it was nice to meet you guys. Thank you for this opportunity. I'll try not to let you down."

♫   ♫   ♫

Sam and Jack knew this would come up at some point, but it's so soon. The fact that Henry has mentioned it is very disappointing. The truth cannot come out.

Amy Strong is the most famous artist ever featured on *Remarkable*. Her season was such a huge success; she became an overnight celebrity. Tragedy ended her dream. In 2003, at the age of nineteen, with the encouragement of her family and friends, she moved to Hollywood to pursue her dreams. Back in San Diego her parents and four of her closest friends were killed in one of the deadliest wildfires to ever hit the California coast. She blamed herself for not being there to help them.

From that moment on, Amy committed all her time and effort to creating an organization that would bring awareness to the dangers of forest fires. She became an environmental activist and left her dreams of becoming an actress behind. She quickly realized that people cared more about the money in their wallets, then they did about the future of our planet. She was vulnerable and alone. Amy wanted to end it all until she found *Remarkable*.

♫   ♫   ♫

As I walk in the door, I feel a lump in my throat. I'm not sure how to tell Rachyl about last night. It's Saturday morning and the house smells of pancakes. The kids are running around playing and Rachyl is on the couch relaxing, phone in hand, checking her feeds. I attempt to give her a kiss on the cheek. She turns her head away.

"No thanks, I'm good. So, how's Maxx doing? Who won the game?"

"You know Maxx, there's always something going on with him, and the Leafs lost as usual."

Only the second part is a lie. There is always something going on with Maxx, that's true, but I have no idea who won the hockey game. I can only assume the Toronto Maple Leafs lost, they usually do.

"Really? It says here the Leafs won."

Of course, she would know the score in the Leaf game today; she never usually does, she hates hockey. The lump in my throat gets bigger as I try to dig myself out,

"You know what, I actually fell asleep before the game was over, they must have come back to win it in the end. They were losing when I fell asleep."

"Interesting. You know what else I saw on here. A trailer for the upcoming season of *Remarkable*. It's about a songwriter from Toronto named Rai Starr. Do you remember that? Or were you fast asleep? Rai, can you please tell me what the hell is going on? Stop lying to me."

"I'm sorry, I didn't fall asleep at Maxx's. I went downtown to the *Remarkable* audition. I didn't want to tell you in case I didn't get the part, I didn't want to disappoint you. Then it got crazy. You guys told me I should do it."

"We have to talk about these things, Rai. You can't just sign up for something like this without telling me. Yes, I said to do it, but not literally the next day. I meant let's talk about it more, you promised me. We have a family, you have an amazing job, do you need this right now? I know you're sad, you miss playing music, I get it. I wish I could go back and change it, but you got sick, life happens. I need you here now, the girls need you, we need Dad."

She's right, I know she is. But I can't stop now, not again. I have to do this for me. I won't be able to live with myself if I quit this time, I have to fight for it.

"I know you do. But, Rach, I need this. I can do both, I promise I'll be here. Things won't get out of hand. It's not that bad anyway. I just go down to their office, they hook me up to this memory machine thing, and it all happens in my head. I'm out of there in a few hours, once a week."

"What memory machine? What are you talking about?" she asks.

"Don't worry, it's safe. I have a guide, a helper, named Henry. He takes care of me. Rach, it's like I'm right back where I was fifteen years ago. You were there, Maxx was there, even June and Dawn were there. I'm back on stage playing music, it's amazing!"

"There are no actors? It's all simulated?" she asks.

"Yes. This guy, Henry, he invented this amazing machine that uses your memory. It's incredible."

"Honestly, the whole thing sounds crazy to me. But you haven't smiled like this in such a long time. If you say it's safe, and this is something you have to do, me and the girls will support you. Just please, be safe."

"I will, thank you, I love you so much."

"I love you more."

Rachyl gets up to check on the kids. I reach into my pocket and grab my phone. How did they make a trailer so fast? I do a quick search and find the trailer. That's when it hits me, this is really happening. It's funny, I'm more nervous about it out here, then I am when I'm in the program. Just then, my phone starts buzzing uncontrollably. I'm getting texts, calls, and notifications from apps I didn't even know I had. I try to look at a few of them, but they just keep rolling in. I've always wondered what a celebrity's cell phone was like. How do they even use it? I shut the phone off and head for the shower. I can't wait for next Friday.

CHAPTER SIX

Henry sinks into his chair. He rubs his eyes; he's physically and mentally exhausted. Only Henry knows the enormity of the world he has created. For the artists in it, and the people watching at home, the program seems insignificant, simply a backdrop for the stories being portrayed. But in reality, the program is a complex coded world, seamlessly combining genuine memory and simulated fantasy. He opens his desk drawer and pulls out a bottle of Jack Daniels. It's the only thing that can take the edge off before he goes back into the program. He pours himself a drink and logs on to his computer. Rai Starr is offline; fortunately for Henry, Rai is not the artist he's searching for. He's looking for Amy

Henry finds Amy's whereabouts in the program and connects himself to his wormhole. Before he enters his codes, he takes a deep breath and prays that this is the visit that brings Amy back.

She is currently wrapping up shooting on an epic film about the life and death of Princess Diana. For the first time in her career, Amy is receiving Oscar buzz for her incredible performance. There's a little coffee shop on set, a place for the actors to relax and unwind. Henry knows she's there, and knows he isn't welcome.

As he approaches the coffee shop, he sees that her agent, Eric Blaze, is there, with Amy. Henry opens the door and sees Eric get up. He has a call. He passes Henry on the way out, and the two men share a glance. Amy looks up at Henry's approach. She sighs.

"What are you doing here, Henry? Can't you ever leave me alone?"

Henry sits down, ignoring Amy's hostility. She's been in the program for two years now and refuses to come out. She is so enthralled with her new life that she has lost touch with reality. If she is forced to leave, Henry is afraid of what she might do to herself. They keep her body in an unmarked room at the end of the hall, separate from the rest.

"You know why I'm here, Amy. This can't go on."

She narrows her eyes. "Why would I leave now? I'm at the pinnacle of my success. I'm Hollywood's hottest actress, and one of the biggest celebrities here."

"You need to stop pushing it, Amy. This isn't real."

Amy basks in the riches of her stardom and often crosses the line between fun and peril. She's addicted to the fame and lives life with reckless abandon because she knows it's all a dream. But what separates a dream from reality if you never wake up?

"You created all this, Henry. Maybe you should take some responsibility for how I am."

If only you knew. I never stop worrying about you, never stop feeling responsible. "I do Amy, that's why I keep coming here every day to bring you back; I'll never give up on you."

Finished with his phone call, Eric gets in between them. "Okay, guys, that's enough. Listen, Henry, obviously this isn't getting anywhere. The movie is almost done, I promise, once we're done shooting, we can all sit down and work out whatever it is you guys are fighting about. Okay? Let me get you guys a coffee."

Henry agrees and Eric leaves to get the coffees. Henry can tell this visit is no different than the rest. Instead of persisting, he changes the subject.

"Anyway, Amy, like I said, the reason I came here is to tell you about this new artist we're featuring, Rai Starr. He's the lead in this amazing band, I really think you'd like his music. It's rock, but with a soulful feel and melody. I brought you a CD of their latest tunes. The band is called Divine Light. Give them a listen and tell me what you think."

Amy takes the CD and looks it over. "Divine Light, cool name. I've been looking for some new music to inspire me. When does he start?"

"Actually, they're playing a show at Lee's Palace around the same time you're in town for the Toronto International Film Festival. You should go check them out."

"Maybe I will."

"Listen, Amy, I know you don't want to leave but I can't do this anymore. You have to come out. This is the last session I'm giving you."

"Henry, enough with this. You promised me you wouldn't pull me until I was ready. I'm not ready."

"There are people in the real world that miss you and care for you. We want you back."

"No one cares about me anymore."

"I do."

Henry backs away slowly as he sees the security guards coming towards him. He quickly makes his way to the back door of the coffee shop and whispers something to Amy. Eric walks back with two hot coffees in his hands, only to see Amy standing alone, and Henry's car squealing away.

"What was that all about?"

"Nothing you have to worry about."

"If it involves you, I will worry about it."

"You're sweet, but all I need you to worry about is me winning that Oscar, the rest, I can take care of myself."

"I believe in you, always."

♫   ♫   ♫

"So, how was it? Tell me about it," Rachyl asks as we finally get some alone time once we get the kids to bed. We unwind on the couch with a couple of hot teas.

"Rach, it's unbelievable. Henry hooks me up to this machine and injects me with this serum. I open my eyes, and I'm on stage. It's our show, the one where we first met."

"I'll never forget that concert. Once I saw you up on that stage, I knew I was going to marry you," Rachyl says with a smile.

"It went very differently this time," I say as I take a long sip.

"What do you mean?"

"Remember your no drug policy? Well, I kind of broke it this time around. I smoked up after the show. I totally freaked out and bailed."

"Rai! How could you?" She gives me a lighthearted punch to the shoulder, making me spill tea on the couch.

"I'm sorry, you'll see once it airs. I didn't mean to, it just happened. I was so worried, but then Henry explained to me that they want the show to be about the music. I hope you don't mind?"

"It's fine, I get it. What else am I gonna see on this show? You better behave yourself."

♫   ♫   ♫

A week has passed in the real world, and I finally get to enter the program for my second session. Henry has everything ready as I anxiously wait to enter.

"Okay, Rai, are you ready?" Henry asks.

"I've been ready since last Friday. It's all I think about. Let's do this."

"Woah, calm down. I know this is exciting Rai, just remember, stay grounded."

I feel the chill of the headset covering my head, triggering goosebumps all down my arms. The warmth of the sedation hits my body and I instantly feel bliss. I close my eyes and enter on a warm summer night in Toronto. We're playing a sold-out show at Lee's Palace concert hall. We take the stage after three of our favorite indie rock bands perform. The show is loud, sweaty, and intense, just the way we like it. The crowd is as loud as ever, and fans try desperately to climb on stage and touch us. Some make it on stage, but security is there to toss them back and send them surfing into the crowd.

After the show, I dry off and walk outside for some cool air. As I light my smoke, I hear a girl's voice behind me.

"Hey, rock star, can I have your autograph?"

I don't recognize her at first, but once I see her long red hair tucked under her cap, I realize it's Amy.

"Only if you give me yours first. You're Amy Strong right?"

I might have been more stunned if I wasn't in the program where I know anything can happen. She looks just like she did in her season.

"Guilty. I'm sorry to creep up on you like a crazy fangirl. Henry from *Remarkable* gave me your CD. I loved it so much I had to come meet you. I've been listening to your songs on repeat for a week. I love them. Not to mention we're in this crazy dream world together."

"Thank you. I know! It's so crazy, isn't it? It feels so real."

"Trust me, the more you're in it, the more real it gets."

"I hope you don't mind me asking, but what happened in your season? Everyone is looking for you. They think you're dead."

"I don't really talk about it with people I don't know."

"What do you say we go for a drink and get to know each other? I have so many questions. I know a bunch of cool bars around here, I'll show you around."

"That sounds fun, okay!"

We talk for hours while bar hopping all night, sharing funny stories, drinking, and enjoying each other's company. Finally, at around two in the morning, Amy begins to open up to me about her personal life. We're the only two people left in the bar and find ourselves sitting closer and closer to each other the longer we talk.

"So, now that we know each other, tell me about yourself. Where did you grow up, what's your story?" I ask.

"Well, let's see. I grew up in San Diego, California. Ever since I can remember I've always wanted to be an actress. But not until my senior year, when I noticed Hollywood agents showing up at my high school plays, did I believe I could do it. They said I had the grace of Audrey Hepburn and the beauty of Sophia Loren. Then, I lost my parents in a forest fire, and suddenly acting wasn't important to me anymore."

"I'm sorry to hear that. I know what that feels like; I lost my father when I was young."

"What about you? Why did you stop playing music?" she asks.

"I was born in Toronto, but I grew up just north of the city. My health is what ended my music dreams. Once I got sick, I had to stop playing."

"That sucks, what was it?"

"It's called ulcerative colitis. Basically, it's a stomach disease. It was tough for me, but I can't imagine how rough it was for you to lose both your parents so suddenly."

I take sip of my Amaro and watch her closely. The way she plays with her hair and bites her lip is irresistible. Before she catches me staring, I say,

"So, tell me, what happened on your season?"

"Once I woke up in here and started acting again, my life finally had purpose again. I was able to save my family this time around, and I quickly realized I never wanted to leave; this is paradise. I found myself wanting more and more time in the program, but Henry wouldn't let me. I'm afraid he's going to pull me out for good. He doesn't understand, an artist's passion is unrelenting. Wouldn't you agree?"

"I do."

She feels the same way I do about the program. Amy is so different than any other girls I've met. She's more confident, independent, and ambitions than I'll ever be; it's alluring.

"Can I trust you, Rai?" she asks.

"I think so; we're having a good time, I feel so comfortable opening up to you. What do you want to tell me?"

"During my season, once I realized this is where I want to be, I started watching Henry closely every time he hooked me up to program. I studied every button he pushed and where he kept all the tools. Eventually, I learned how the program works and how to operate all the machines. I've come up with a plan on how to get more time in the program, but I need someone to help me. Henry is wary of me, I need someone he won't suspect. Will you help me?"

"That's a big ask, Amy. I want to help you, but I'm just getting started. I don't want to mess up this opportunity."

Amy moves her bar stool closer and says, "I know it's a lot to ask, but it's something we both want. You may not feel it now, but you will. The more time you spend in here, the more time you'll crave. I'm in town for a while promoting my movie. Come visit me at my hotel when you're ready. Promise me you'll at least think about it?" Amy leans in and kisses me on the cheek. I look into her eyes and kiss her softly on her lips.

We leave the bar and continue kissing in the cab. We reach her hotel and I exit the cab to open her door. "I had such a great time tonight. Thank you for coming to find me."

"The night doesn't have to be over, Rai." She walks toward the hotel doors, turns back, and says, "Well, are you coming up?"

I close the cab door and follow her up to her suite.

♫   ♫   ♫

Thanks to the news of us being pursued by a major label, our shows have been sold out and the buzz around us is at an all-time high. After weeks of deliberating, the band finally agrees to discuss a contract with Reckless Records.

Doug is sitting across from us while a young Jack Cranney sits at the head of the boardroom table. The recording contracts are laid out in front of us and Doug begins to read.

"Okay, gentlemen, this is your recording contract. It's a three-album deal, with Reckless Records owning fifty percent of the music and royalties, while the remaining fifty percent is split evenly amongst the four of you."

I look at Maxx and shake my head. He looks back at me and motions for me to stop. Doug continues.

"You will embark on a full North American tour once the first album is recorded. The studio is booked to begin recording next week - Metalworks Studios in Mississauga. Your signing bonus today is ten thousand dollars each, and all other expenses related to the recording and the tour are to be taken from your end of the royalties."

"Fifty-one percent," I say.

"Excuse me, what was that, Rai?" Doug asks.

"We want to own fifty-one percent of the music and we're not paying a penny for the recording or the tour."

"Well, Rai. It costs a lot of money and takes a tremendous amount of effort to record an album and put on a tour. We think our offer is more than fair."

"I really don't care about what you think. This is our music and we want to own the majority share. Non-negotiable."

The room gets eerily quiet. Maxx looks at me with wide eyes, while the rest of the guys have their heads down. Doug looks at Jack in disbelief. Jack sits up in his chair and breaks the silence.

"Okay, guys let's all relax here. I understand that you feel like we're taking something away from you, but trust me, we're not. These are standard contracts that all our acts sign. We're willing to split the costs of the tour and recordings as a sign of good faith. Doug here is a great agent and has all your best interests in mind."

"Oh really? Is that why he didn't even remember the band's name after our show? I guarantee you he can't name three of our songs."

"Stop, just wait a second." Maxx speaks as he gets up off his chair. "Rai, can I talk to you outside for a minute?"

Maxx walks toward the door and waits for me to meet him out in the hallway. I push back my chair and follow him. I can sense that Maxx is not happy. As soon as the door closes behind me, Maxx starts screaming at me.

"What the hell is wrong with you? Are you trying to sabotage this whole thing for all of us?"

"I never agreed to those terms. I knew they were going to try and screw us, don't you see that?"

"Calm down, man. Look, this is our shot. Not too many people are lucky enough to get an opportunity like this. Let's get back in there, sign the deal, and do this together as a band."

"Maybe I don't want be in this band anymore."

"Oh really? What are you going to do, quit now, just as we're about to sign a record deal? What, are you crazy?"

"Maybe I am crazy, but I know one thing, I'm not going to bend over to some record company and give away all my music."

"Your music? I see now. You think this is all your music and we're nothing without you. Doug told me this was going to happen, but I didn't believe him. He knew you would do this. He said at some point you were going to think you were too good for us and would want to go solo."

"Maxx, that's not what I meant. Let's just get out of here and sign with SubRock. Dani was great, man, she cared about us. We would have all the control over what we do. We're slaves if we stay here. They're going to own all the music and make all the money, while we bust our ass on tour."

"No way, man, we're signing with Reckless, with or without you. If you don't like it, you can leave."

I stare at Maxx with rage in my eyes as my blood begins to boil. I shove his chest as hard as I can, hurling him backwards. His body smashes against the wall leaving a large dent, knocking two gold records off the wall. My hands are stinging from the force of the blow. Maxx bounces off the wall and lunges towards me. We fall backward onto an office plant; soil spills across the room, as two security guards come running into the hallway to break it up. I manage to wiggle away, swing open the boardroom door, and announce my intentions.

"Good luck, boys, I quit."

I storm out of the building and jump on the nearest streetcar. If it's entertainment Sam and Jack Cranney want, they got it. This is my dream after all. I'm going to do this my way. I reach into my pocket and pull out Dani's card. Next stop, SubRock Records.

CHAPTER SEVEN

As soon as I reach the SubRock offices, I instantly feel more at home. The two companies couldn't be more different. The Reckless building is on Bay Street, which is known as the financial district, whereas SubRock is in Queen West, where you can find all the best art, food, and music anywhere in Toronto. The SubRock office is on the third floor of an old commercial building. There's no billboard, or golden statue out front, just a small simple neon sign with their name and logo.

I walk in the door and see no desk, no coffee table, or receptionist. Instead, there's a few couches, guitar stools, and swivel chairs surrounding a handcrafted wooden table. There are no doors on the offices so people can walk freely from space to space. There is a large bookshelf on which are hundreds of old records, and a record player spinning classic 60s rock tunes. A woman walks by me with a stack of folders in her hands; she's the only one who looks like she's working.

"Hi, I'm looking for Dani. Is she here?"

"Yeah, she's in Studio A, just down that hall, you can't miss it. Hey, you're in Divine Light, right?"

"I am. Yeah. Actually, I was."

"Really? Well, I love your music, we all do. I'm glad you're here. I'm Candice, Dani's assistant. Everyone calls me Candi. Wow, Dani was right, you are cute."

I laugh nervously and shake her hand. "Hi Candi, I'm Rai. This place is amazing, I love the vibe."

"Don't let the laid-back atmosphere fool you; there's some amazing work being done here, you'll see. Studio A is right down that hall; she might be in with an artist, just wave from the window, she'll come out."

I walk down the hallway and admire all the artwork pinned to the wall. It's littered with cool fanzines and concert posters from one of my favorite local artists, Robb Mirsky. At the end of the surprisingly quiet hall, there's a huge window with two doors on either side. The door to the left is marked Studio A, which the large window appears to look in to. There's a session going on with three musicians; two guys and a girl. It's dimly lit and hard to make out who they are. I see Dani off to the side tapping on a tambourine; she glances over, waves and motions for me to come in.

As I open the door, the sound from inside fills the silence in the hall. The room is so loud. I walk in unnoticed, as the three musicians are lost in the music. The two guys are playing acoustic guitars, while the girl is handling the main vocals. Her voice has a beautifully soft, but raspy tone, which is heightened by the enchanting guitars and mesmerizing background vocals. Dani comes close and says,

"Let's talk outside."

"Okay."

Dani opens the studio door and we walk into the silence of the hallway. Once the door closes, I turn to Dani with wide eyes.

"Is that Gord Downie? Dallas Green? And Emily Haines from Metric?"

"Yeah. Emily and Gord are helping Dallas with his new solo record. He wants to do something a little more personal when he's not with Alexisonfire."

"Are they're going to do an album together? That's going to be huge. I thought you were just a small up and coming label."

"No, they're not collaborating, they're just helping each other out, that's what artists do. They're not signed to our label. They just needed a low-key place to jam. Dallas is an old high school friend of mine and asked me if I had some space."

"That's amazing. We just played a show with Alexisonfire, but I didn't get to meet him."

"I know, Dallas told me, he really liked you guys. Let's go in Studio B. We can talk in private and I can show you the equipment."

Studio B is much smaller. There are a few guitars on stands against the wall and an old piano tucked in the corner of the room. The microphones are older, but still in great condition. There's a smaller mixing room to the side where the recording equipment sits, and a bunch of soundproofing panels all over the walls. We sit on guitar stools in the middle of the room and chat.

"So, Rai. It's nice to see you. I have to say, I didn't think I'd ever see you again once that Reckless agent got his hands on you. I'm surprised."

"You shouldn't be, I told you I'd be right back. It just took a little longer then I thought. I want to work with you."

"Really, what do the other guys think? I thought I lost you?"

"Well, you did lose Divine Light, but you didn't lose me. It's over, I left. I couldn't do it. I couldn't let those corporate leeches suck the life out of my music. I tried to convince the guys, but they were hooked. Money is a crazy motivator for them."

"Wow, that's a big decision. Good for you. It takes a lot of guts to go out on your own, I'm impressed. I'm sorry I left without

saying goodbye at your show. I was hurt, but I'm glad you're here."
Dani gives me a hug. "So, tell me, what do you wanna do?"

"Well, I've always had these acoustic songs that I love but
weren't quite right for the band. I'd like to record those and see how
they sound, just me and my acoustic guitar."

"I like that idea, let's hear some songs."

"What, now?"

"Yeah, why not?" Dani hands me a guitar and heads over to
the mixing room to turn everything on. Once everything is rolling,
she walks over to the piano bench and listens. I look down at the
guitar and start to feel nervous. I've never played these songs in
front of anyone before. These are the songs I play when I'm feeling
lost. They're all about my personal feelings, experiences, and
relationships. I close my eyes and start to play a song called *Bad
Ones*. The room sounds amazing; it sounds so full and it carries the
music so beautifully. I finish my song and look over at Dani, who's
smiling.

"Rai, I love it."

"Thanks."

"Try another one. Do you mind if I play a little piano?"

"Not at all. This one's called *Been Through*."

I get lost in the music for a while. We play a few more tunes
and really start to feel it. Suddenly, I hear a gentle voice humming a
beautiful background melody, and two guitars strumming along in
perfect harmony. I open my eyes and find myself in the middle of a
jam session with Gord, Dallas, and Emily. I can't believe how good
it sounds and how they're able to pick up the chords so quickly. I
feel like I'm floating as I play my music with my heroes. The song
ends and I'm speechless. Gord Downie is sitting right beside me.

"That was great, man," he says.

"Thank you, I can't believe you guys are here."

"We were about to leave when Dani called us in to have a listen. It sounded so pure and honest, we had to join in. I hope you don't mind," Emily says.

"Not at all. I'm such a huge fan of all you guys. Thank you so much."

"Don't thank us, thank Dani. She's amazing, be good to her," Dallas says. "See you next week, Dani, thanks for the jam, Rai Starr, good luck with your album, can't wait to hear it."

Gord, Emily and Dallas leave, and I can't stop smiling. Like a thirteen-year-old fanboy, I'm slightly freaking out. It feels so real, even though I know it isn't. Gord Downie died in 2017. I remember watching his final concert with The Tragically Hip and feeling so sad that we lost a legend. Dani comes over and sits on the guitar stool next to me.

"So, how does it feel to play with your heroes?"

I'm at a loss for words. "It feels…so… inspiring. And you, on the piano, were amazing. How did you learn to play like that?"

"Thanks. I play a little. That's what three years of piano lessons gets you, which I hated. But as I got older, I appreciated it more and more, that's when I fell in love with music. So, what do you think? Are you ready to record with SubRock?"

"Only if you promise to play piano on the record."

"Deal, let's make a record."

We shake hands, but she doesn't let go. She gives me a look, pulls me close, and says, "I'm so happy you're here, I thought I'd never see you again." She kisses me on the cheek. I freeze.

"Dani, you're an amazing girl. But I came here because I want to record with someone who understands and loves music as much as I do. Let's just focus on that, okay."

"You're right, I'm sorry. I got caught up in the moment. Give me a couple days to set up, then I'll call you and we can get started."

I leave SubRock and make my way back to the unit feeling exhausted. I've been crashing here while in the program. My eyes begin to close as the serum wears off. As I lay on the couch and begin to fall asleep, I think, this is it, this is my dream. All I want to do is make this record and hear my songs on the radio. I need to prove to myself that I can do it, that I'm good enough. Amy is right, I want more time.

♫   ♫   ♫

Waking up in the real world gets more and more frustrating. I have so much I want to do back in the program that it consumes my thoughts. Also, since the first few episodes of *Remarkable* aired, it's getting harder and harder for me to go anywhere without being recognized. Every time I go anywhere, there are paparazzi waiting for me. I used to stop and chat, take a few pictures, and leave. But now it's just relentless, getting more and more irritating and invasive. As soon as I step out of the Reckless building, I see a crowd forming, cameras flashing, and microphones in hand.

"Rai Starr, Rai Starr, how do you feel about the news breaking this hour?" a journalist asks.

"What news is that?" I ask, looking forward and walking swiftly towards the limo, with my bodyguard beside me.

"The estate representing Amy Strong has just filed a lawsuit against Reckless Records. They claim that she's alive, and that the company is covering up her whereabouts. Do you have any comment?"

The press is always asking me outlandish questions, today is no different. But this time, they're actually on to something. I play it off as best as I can.

"It's not my place to comment on things that I'm not involved in, that has nothing to do with my season. It doesn't make much sense to me though, why would they do something like that?"

"Some are saying that the actors portraying your characters in the show are not actors at all, but it's actually a simulation. They're using a computer program to mess with your memories, and she may be trapped in a virtual word."

"Honestly, that seems a little farfetched. It's a tragedy what happened to Amy, her family and friends have been through enough, let them have their peace. I wouldn't fall for these conspiracy theories."

"Then why haven't any of the actors in the show come forward? Have you met the actor that plays you in the show?"

"If there's a lawsuit happening, I don't think I should comment on any of this; if you wanna talk about my season, I'd be more than happy to, but I have to go."

"Rai! Rai! Over here. Last question. A lot of people are saying you left the band and signed with SubRock because you're in love with the owner, Dani. Some sources are saying that they've seen you, outside of the show, holding hands and coddling with a woman who looks like Dani. Is that true?"

"You guys are crazy, this is show business. The stories in the show are just what would have happened if I continued with my music career. There is no real-life Dani. I can assure you, I am a happily married man, that's all there is to it. I have to go."

Just then, Henry pulls up and motions for me to get in his car. The sounds of screaming reporters and flashing lights fade as I jump in and we pull away from the building. Things are getting crazy. All I can think about is that moment in Studio B with Dani. Nothing happened, but it didn't look good, and now all this. I just hope Rachyl isn't falling for this tabloid garbage. I wish I could leave this chaos and just go back in the program. I turn to Henry.

"Henry, this is crazy. Rachyl is going to kill me! Is it all over the papers? I can't go anywhere with these people asking all these questions. I just want to stay in the program, play my music, and forget all this."

"Don't fall for all this hype, Rai. I know it's hard for you to see right now, but the world doesn't revolve around you. That being said, celebrity is big business. People want to know about the hottest celebrities, and the tabloids want to sell papers, this is part of the deal. I told you, fame can be a dangerous thing, if you let it."

"And why am I getting all these questions about that Amy girl? You know they're suing you right? And why don't they know about the program? I want to know everything, right now."

"Okay, calm down. I didn't want to bother you with these issues, but if you must know, then here it is. The program wasn't exactly universally accepted by the powers that be when I first presented it. Jack promised me he would get approval from the FCC, and everything would be fine, but he never did. Then, once we started airing, and we got so big that the money started flowing in, the FCC stopped asking questions and the problem went away; that's the last I heard about it until now."

"Why wasn't it approved?"

"The FCC collaborated with some scientists and concluded that creating a virtual world was unstable. If it got into the wrong hands, it could lead to addiction and mass exile to this new dream world. But I know the scientists they talked to. They're just bitter that I came up with this program before they did. It's all a ruse to discredit my life's work."

"And what about Amy, Henry? Where is she?"

"Honestly, I don't know."

The thoughts running through my head are overwhelming. This is too much to process right now, I just want to get home. I'm so mad at Henry right now. If he lied about the program, what else is he lying about.

I keep quiet as we drive to my home in the suburbs. As we approach my house, we notice a commotion, so Henry stops the car on the corner of the street. The scene in front of my house is unbelievable. My driveway is overrun by paparazzi and news reporters. I can see the fear on the faces of Rachyl and the kids, peeking through the bedroom curtains.

"This is your life now, Rai. As I said before you agreed to do this, you will transform from someone with little means, to an instant celebrity."

I get out of the car and slam the door behind me. The flashing lights are disorienting as I fight my way through the crowd. The screaming questions are just noise as I make it to the front door. Rachyl is there waiting for me. She opens and closes the door in a hurry as I rush in.

"Rai, this is crazy. We can't live like this, we have a family. We can't even leave our house."

"I know, I'm sorry. It's getting out of hand. I'll figure something out. Don't worry. Are you guys okay?"

"We're fine, just a little shaken up. Something happened last night, Rai." Rachyl speaks quietly, making sure the girls can't hear from upstairs. "I was tucking the girls in last night and dozed off in Nellie's bed. When I woke up to go back to our room, I heard something outside. I looked through the window and saw some crazy fan girl trying to open our back door; she was wearing a Divine Light t-shirt and whispering your name. I was so scared, Rai."

I can't believe this got out of hand so quickly. I've heard of an overnight success, but this is ridiculous. I never want to put my family in danger. I don't know what to say, I don't know what to do.

"What if she'd got in the house, Rai? Not to mention, the girls are always asking what's wrong with you. We miss you, you're here, but your mind is there all the time, and now I'm hearing these crazy rumors about another girl. I can't do this, I want our old life back. I don't care about any of this, I just want you back." Rachyl storms upstairs.

There's a knock on the door. I look through the peephole and see Henry standing on the porch hiding his face from the cameras. I quickly open the door and pull him inside.

"Rai, I'm sorry, I couldn't leave without telling you. I know I haven't been completely honest with you about the program and the show, but you have to trust me. I'm trying to do the right thing, I just need some time."

"First, I want you to get security over here every night. Rachyl and the kids are scared, and I don't blame them." I can feel my chest getting tight. I take a few deep breaths and try to breathe. My anxiety is back, the real world is suffocating, I need to get out of here. "And I want to go back in, tonight. I can't handle this. I need to play some music and clear my head."

"Rai, you can't escape your reality; I know you want to, but I've seen this before with other artists. Some of them get too comfortable in the program. They begin to lose track of reality. I don't want that to happen to you, like it did to…"

Just then Rachyl and the girls come down the stairs to see who I'm talking to. She cuts Henry off mid-sentence. "Rai who is this, and why are they in our house?"

"It's okay, Rach, this is Henry. Henry, this is my wife, Rachyl, and my kids, Nellie and Aly. Guys, this is Henry, he works at Remarkable, he's my guide."

"Hi, everyone, it's nice to finally meet you. Rai talks about you guys a lot. It's nice to put a face to the names."

"Sorry, it's nice to meet you too, say hi guys." The kids stay quiet and hide behind their mother. "They're just a little shy right now," Rachyl says.

"It's okay. Rachyl, here's my card. I'd like to connect with you and discuss any questions or concerns you may have. I know this is a crazy time and I'd love to get the chance to talk."

"I definitely will, thank you. I'll leave you two alone, come on guys, let's go up." Rachyl and the kids make their way upstairs. Once they're out of sight, I ask Henry,

"When can we go in tonight?"

"Slow down, Rai, you just got out. This is also why I came back. You're starting to slip. You keep asking me to go back in when you're not scheduled. Stay here and talk to Rachyl and your kids. They need you right now. We'll go back next Friday when you're scheduled."

"I can't wait that long, Henry. I'm going in tonight. Or else I'll start talking to the press. I talked to Amy, I know what's going on, Henry."

"What do you mean? I don't know what you're talking about."

"You know exactly what I mean, Henry. Amy is in a hidden chamber at Reckless, she won't come out of the program. You can't live with the fact that your program did this to her, that's why you keep trying to get her to come out before it's too late. Sam and Jack are keeping her alive until her story blows over, then they'll pull her plug."

"Rai, she's sick, you don't understand."

"I completely understand. This is what's going to happen; I'm going to stay here with Rachyl and the kids, then, once everyone is asleep, I'm going to meet you at the Reckless building. You're going to put me back in so I can finish my album."

"You don't leave me with much choice, do you? I will, on one condition, I will only give enough serum for a one-hour session, that will give you enough time to finish your album and come out safe."

"Deal."

Henry opens the door and covers his face so the cameras can't identify him. I make my way upstairs. I call a family meeting in our bedroom. Everyone walks in and sits on the bed. Rachyl has her arms crossed, and the kids are quiet. I can feel the tension in the room.

"Okay, guys, I'm sorry that all this has gotten out of control. I've asked Henry to get us some extra security at the house so nothing crazy happens. I promise this will be all over soon and we can go back to normal."

After a minute of silence, Nellie asks, "When can we play outside again? I wanna ride my bike and play with my friends."

"I know, Nells, of course, honey, once the nice people come and protect us, you can go outside and play all day, okay?"

"Okay, Daddy," she says, but I can see the worry in her eyes, and in all their eyes.

"You know what I'm gonna do, I'm gonna buy a big swing set and playground for the backyard. You can invite all your friends over and have lots of fun. How does that sound?"

"And a treehouse," Aly says.

"The biggest treehouse you've ever seen." I jump on the bed and tickle the kids until I get a laugh and we come together for a long family hug. The kids go running off to finish playing their game, while Rachyl and I finish talking.

"You better come through with that treehouse, or I'll never hear the end of it."

"I know, I will. Are you okay?"

"I feel a little better now that I've met Henry. At least I know someone is taking care of you and watching out for us. I just don't want you to have any regrets. We've come this far. I know how much this means to you, and I want you to be happy. Are you happy?"

"I feel like I will be soon. Once I do this and heal my past, I can come out and be a better husband, a better dad, and a better person. I won't have this weight of "what if" heavy on my shoulders. I can enjoy my life with you and the kids, that's what I want. You and the kids deserve that."

♫   ♫   ♫

It's one o'clock in the morning as I reach the Reckless front gates. I wait for Henry as patiently as I can. My legs are moving uncontrollably, and I can't stop tapping my fingers. I hate waiting, where is he? The gates finally open and I see Henry holding a door open for me.

"I don't like coming here on off-scheduled days. Sam and Jack might be watching. You don't know what they're capable of. I'm serious, Rai, never again."

Henry unlocks the door to the chamber and begins to start up the computers and warm up the machines. After I get undressed, I sneak out and start to look around to find the zip ties. I know he keeps them in the storage room. I open a few cupboards and drawers but find nothing. I look on the shelf where he keeps the garbage bags and see the zip ties stacked up beside them. I grab a few and scrunch them in the palm of my right hand.

I walk back into the chamber and head straight for the chair. I lie back with my right arm hanging over the side, opposite Henry. He reaches for the sedation gas mask and slowly moves toward me. I lunge and grab his wrist and force the mask over his face. I hold it there with all my strength until I feel no resistance. Henry's eyes slowly fade as he gradually falls to his knees. I grab his arms and wrap them behind his back and zip tie them securely to the sturdy legs of his desk.

I walk through the opposing door and down the hallway to the unmarked chamber where Amy told me her body is kept. She's thin and pale. You can tell she hasn't moved in months. There's a bed bath station beside her chair and a tray piled with empty saline bags. She said Henry keeps the serum in the fridge against the back wall. I grab two syringes, one for me, and one for Amy. I inject Amy with a maximum dose of serum and head back to my chamber.

I pull out the notes Amy had written for me and search for her location in the program; I find her, and enter the codes. I only have a few seconds to inject the serum after I take the sedation. I lay back on the chair and begin to breathe in the gas. I count to five and slowly inject the serum. My eyes close and I begin to drift away.

I enter the program in front of the Fox Theatre in downtown Toronto. Amy is premiering her Oscar-nominated movie, *The Heart of a Princess*. I spot Amy in the crowd of celebrities. She looks stunning in her long white gown and her jewelry sparkling in the flashing lights of the cameras. She meets me in the VIP area.

"Hey, movie star, you look amazing."

"Thank you, what are you doing here?"

"It's done. Henry will be out of the picture for a while and you're fully loaded." Before I can finish speaking, a sharp-dressed man with a neatly trimmed beard stands between us.

"Sorry, this is Eric, he's my agent. Eric, this is Rai Starr."

Eric eyes me down, forces a fake smile, and firmly shakes my hand. "Nice to meet you, Rai; we've been listening to some of your tunes, sounds great."

"Thanks." I switch my attention to Amy. "I can't wait to see the movie, I'm sure it's amazing. I'm gonna go. This is a big night for you; I just wanted to tell you the good news. Call me later and we can hang out."

"Thank you, Rai, I can't wait to hear your new record. You're gonna be a rock star, start living like one."

Amy makes a move to kiss me, but Eric is there to shut it down. He grabs her by the arm and pulls her away. "Come on, Amy, we have to go in, the screening is starting."

Amy waves goodbye and disappears into the herd of reporters and celebrities.

CHAPTER EIGHT

Henry opens his eyes and feels the heavy drowse of the sedation. He tries to pull himself up when he notices he's been restrained. It's hard for him to remember what happened, but he knows this could only be caused by an addict. He knew the addiction was getting worse but didn't think it would escalate to this. He tries desperately to free himself from the desk, but he's too weak to move. His phone vibrates on his desk above him. He uses all the strength he has to get to his feet. He looks over his shoulders and sees the call display, it's Rachyl. He manages to answer, using his pinky finger.

"Hello, Rachyl."

"Hi, is this Henry?"

"Yes. Yes, it is."

"I'm sorry to call you so late, but I woke up in the middle of the night and Rai was gone; do you know where he is?"

"I do. Please come down to the office, something happened, Rai's in trouble. I need your help."

Rachyl jumps out of bed and rushes to get dressed. She calls June. "June, Rai's in trouble, I need you to come watch the kids, I'll explain once I get back, please hurry."

"I'm coming right now, Rach."

Once June arrives, Rachyl runs to the car and speeds to the Reckless building. As soon as Rachyl reaches the offices, she calls Henry in a panic.

"Henry I'm here, what do I do?"

"Go around to the left side of the building, you'll see a door that says authorized personnel only. Do you see it"

"I can't see anything, it's pitch black out here. Wait, I see it, I see it."

"Okay, on the doorknob you'll see a keypad, enter 0319, the door should unlock."

Rachyl's hand trembles as she enters the code. "Okay, okay, I'm in. Where do I go now?" she asks.

"To your right, you'll see a long hallway with double doors at the end. Enter the same code and the doors will open, I'm in the first office on the right."

Rachyl enters the chamber and sees Rai's body hooked up to the machine and lets out a loud scream. She sees Henry tied to his desk and rushes over and tries to untie him. Her hands are fumbling in shock as she comes to grips with what's unfolding in front of her.

"Henry, what's going on?"

"It's Rai, he's in trouble. He's worse than I thought. He drugged me and went into the program himself. He's addicted to his life in there. He's working with Amy."

"What do we do?"

"Untie me, I have an idea. You're the only one who can help him now. Rachyl...you're going in."

♫　　♫　　♫

It's a confusing time in the program for me right now. I can't get Amy off my mind, but I also find myself thinking about Dani, and our moment in Studio B. Amy is wild and exciting, Dani is smart and ambitious. Even though I'm trying to focus on the music right now, I just can't help myself.

I booked two weeks of studio time to record my debut solo album. Dani has everything set up for me to do my thing. The mics are hanging from the ceiling to capture the amazing acoustics and all my guitars are ready on their stands. There are violet lilies and white candles arranged throughout the room to set the mood. It's exactly how I've always envisioned it would be. I settle onto my guitar stool while Dani rustles her music sheets at the piano. I start with a few strums of my guitar and Dani follows with subtle notes from the piano that elegantly fill the background. We play for hours, getting lost in the music.

We record about twelve songs, but I know I only want ten on the album. Choosing which ten is an impossibility for me. Another byproduct of my insecurities is the inability to know which one of my songs is better or worse than another. I don't think any one song can be better than another, just like I don't think one painting can be better than another painting. In my mind art can only be different, not better, or worse. So, I decide to leave that up to Dani. She has a great ear for that kind of thing. The more time I spend with her, the more I like her. I feel so comfortable when I'm with her. Even though we've just met, it's like we've known each other for years. I'm falling for her.

We finish up for the day and go over some of the changes we want to make in the mixing room.

"Rai, your voice sounded so beautiful today. So sincere and pure."

"Thanks, I have good and bad days. Luckily today was a good day."

Dani looks down at my lips while she bites hers. She leans in for a kiss. We close our eyes as our lips meet, and a familiar feeling fills my body. We stare at each other for a while, holding hands. She looks at me the same way Rachyl looks at me. She pulls me close and leans in for another kiss. I quickly realize that everyone is watching at home, including Rachyl, so I pull away. She catches herself and says,

"I'm sorry, I didn't mean to…"

Just then, Candi knocks on the mixing room door. Dani backs away from me as she enters the room.

"Hey guys, I hope I'm not interrupting?"

"No, it's okay, we're just finishing up," Dani replies.

"You guys sound so good. Is *Poor Suffering Me* going to be on the album? I love that song."

"Thanks, I'm not sure. You'll have to ask Dani, I hate choosing,"

Dani smiles at me as I give her a friendly shove. She looks different today; her hair's a little longer and her eyes look a little more emerald than blue, maybe it's the light in the studio. I gaze at Dani a little too long; thankfully, Candi breaks the silence.

"Dani, I came in to let you know that Jeremy just dropped off two tickets to the Our Lady Peace concert tonight. I can't go, I have that lame wedding reception tonight, so they're all yours."

"Awesome. Rai, you wanna go?" Dani asks.

"I'd love to, where's it at? Who's the opening act?"

"It's at the Mod Club and I'm not sure who's opening, it doesn't say, it just says special guests," Candi says.

"Okay, great. Thanks, Candi, we'll take them. You know what, take the weekend off, enjoy yourself."

"Sounds good to me, see you Monday. Have fun, guys."

♫   ♫   ♫

Dani and I share a cab down to the Mod Club Theatre in Toronto's Little Italy. I've always wanted to play here but never got the chance to. We're early, yet the line to get in is huge, so we walk around a bit and find a little Italian café for a coffee and sweets. It looks like it's been here for generations. There are Italian flags everywhere, Sinatra playing in the background, and signs claiming they have the best cannoli in town.

There are a few older men having coffee at the bar, and a pleasant older Italian lady serving behind the counter. I order an espresso and a chocolate cannoli. Dani skips coffee and goes straight for the gelato bar. She orders two scoops of pistachio ice cream in a waffle cone.

"Thank you," Dani says as she reaches for the ice cream.

"My pleasure, dear. It brings me great joy to serve people in love."

"Oh, we are not a couple, we work together," Dani replies.

"Ah, I see. I'm sorry, I'm not usually wrong about these things. Enjoy your ice cream."

We take our order to go and stand in the line for about ten minutes before I notice the sign. I look up and let out a sarcastic chuckle as I see who the opening act is. Of course it's them. I motion for Dani to look up at the sign. It reads, "Our Lady Peace" in big bold letters, and "with Divine Light" in small block letters below.

"Oh my God, I'm so sorry. I had no idea. We can go."

"No way, are you kidding me? I have to see this."

"Are you sure? I don't care. I've seen Our Lady Peace so many times."

"Honestly, it's okay. Let's just enjoy our night, I'll be fine."

The Mod Club is an intimate venue with a small stage and long narrow bar along one side. There's an upper level where the dressing rooms are and a balcony where the bands can hang out and watch the other performers. The place is packed, and I notice a few fans wearing Divine Light t-shirts. I guess selling out to a big record company does have its perks. Money and influence can buy you a lot of things in the music industry. Maybe I'm a little jealous, but their fans seem so manufactured.

We find a good spot by the bar and order a couple of beers. Dani looks amazing. She has such a great style and presence. I feel so comfortable around her. Even when I'm not in the program, I find myself thinking about her a lot. We clink our beers and turn to the stage; the show is about to start.

It begins with some familiar chords and a loud roar from the crowd. Maxx is the front man now. He's dressed all in black and is playing a bright red Gibson SG bass with a lighting strap. Higgins and Rikki sound tight; it's too bad I can't say the same for Maxx. He seems sluggish and sloppy. I'm not sure if he changed some of the words, or he can't remember them, not to mention his voice sounds awful. The crowd doesn't seem to notice, but what do they know? Dani says they sound okay, but nothing like when we were all together. Divine Light was never intended to be a three-piece band. In order to get the right sound, you need a second guitar for fills and harmonies. As good as Higgins is on guitar, it's just too much to handle. Divine Light finishes their set and Our Lady Peace takes the stage. They sound great, just like I remember. They were a big influence musically, and one of my favorite Canadian bands.

After the show, I catch up with a few of the roadies and manage to make it backstage. Higgins is toweling off, while Rikki is chugging a bottle of water. Maxx is nowhere to be found. I walk behind Higgins and tap him on the shoulder.

"Hey, man. You guys sounded great. How've you guys been?"

"Starr! I didn't know you were coming. Thanks, man, things are crazy busy. We're playing so many shows, the days are just flying by." He gives me a big hug.

"That's good to hear, man. Where's Maxx?"

"Maxx is somewhere, we don't see him much." Rikki comes over and joins us.

"Listen, guys, I just want to say, I'm sorry for ditching like that. I'm sure Maxx said something about it, but I just wanted you guys to know, it wasn't anything you did. I just didn't like the direction things were going."

"We get it, man. To be honest, things aren't exactly what we expected. We're on the road a lot. New shows keep popping up. We're exhausted," Rikki says, looking depleted. "Have you spoken to Maxx?"

"Nah, I haven't seen him in a while. We didn't exactly leave on good terms."

"He's different now. Ever since that day at the meeting he's changed. He's by himself a lot. We see him at rehearsal, then at the show, and that's it. He's lost a lot of weight, he hangs out with these sketchy dudes, and he struggles on stage at times. We're worried," Rikki says.

"That doesn't sound good. I've seen those signs before, it usually doesn't end well. I'll try and talk to him. Is he around?"

"I don't think that's such a good idea," Higgins says.

"Why not?"

"Anytime we even mention your name, he loses it. He's pissed at you, man. I would avoid him at all costs. There's no telling what he'll do anymore."

I knew he would be upset, but not this much. At the end of the day, he's still my friend and I'm worried about the path he's on. If what the guys are saying is true, it can only mean one thing: heroin. I must admit, I have considered trying it in the past. When my stomach was really bad and nothing seemed to work, I wanted to try it. All my idols were doing it, and I thought it could help ease my pain and stress. Thankfully, I decided to go to the doctor instead of self-medicating.

"Where is he?"

"If he's still here, he'll be in the dressing room upstairs with his entourage," Higgins says.

I walk up the dimly-lit staircase and make my way to the grungy dressing room. I knock on the door a few times, but there's no answer. I knock a little harder until finally someone answers.

"Who are you?" a young girl asks as she peeks through the door.

"I'm looking for Maxx."

"Maxx, some guy is asking for you, what do you want me to tell him?"

I can see Maxx through the crack in the door; he leans over and looks towards us. He looks even worse offstage. His eyes are bloodshot and he's shockingly thin. I can see drug paraphernalia littered all over the table. He quickly covers his stash and gets up. He takes a swig of his beer, walks to the door, and pushes the girl aside.

"Who the hell let you in here? You're not welcome. This area is for bands only, you quit this band, remember?"

"Look, man, I don't want any trouble, I just want to make sure you're okay."

"You got a lot of nerve coming here after what you did to us. I should smash this bottle over your head. I'm fine; leave me alone. We're better without you anyway."

"Listen, man, whatever you're doing, stop. These dopeheads you're hanging out with, they're not your friends. They're just using you. Look at you, you look terrible, man."

"You lost your right to tell me what to do when you left this band. This is my band now, I'll do what I want."

"Funny, it still sounds like my band. All the songs you sang tonight are mine; have you even written an original song since I left?"

"According to our contact, they're our songs now; next time read the fine print."

"You know what, you can have them; you're going to need them more than I do. I know I can write more, I doubt you can now."

Maxx shoves me as hard as he can and slams the door in my face. There's no hope, he's lost. I make my way back downstairs and find the rest of the band.

"Higgs, Rikki, sorry guys, I'm out of here. I know when I'm not wanted. Maxx is in deep, I can see it in his eyes. He needs help. I know it's tough, but you have to tell the record company, they can get him help. He needs rehab."

"We tried, they don't care. As long as we're playing shows and making money, they won't do anything. Every time we tell them, they say they're working on it, but they never follow through," Rikki says.

"I don't know what to say, guys, I tried. Just keep an eye on him. Hopefully, it's just a phase and he can get his act together."

I finish my goodbyes and go back into the crowd to find Dani. Our Lady Peace has come back to do their encore. I find Dani in the pit and motion to her that I want to leave. It's so loud down here, I can't hear a word she's saying. She mouths back,

"One more song."

I nod my head, fight my way through the crowd, and stand behind her. Our Lady Peace sound great. I've seen them a bunch of times and they never disappoint; Rachyl loves them too. But still, all I can think about is Maxx. It's crazy, I know this is all fake, but my emotions are so real. The band finishes up and walks offstage. I grab Dani's hand and we head for the door.

♫   ♫   ♫

The next few weeks in the program are exhilarating. Dani decides to release a single before my album is done to see what kind of response we get. The song she chooses is *I Must Be Crazy* - it goes viral. Everywhere I go in the program, I'm mobbed by people trying to get a piece of me.

The more famous I get, the more I find myself hanging out with Amy. She takes me to all her private parties, and we chill with all her celebrity friends. I'm definitely living like a rock star now.

I haven't been seeing Dani much. She's been busy mixing and promoting the album. Dani calls sometimes and pleads with me to get back in the studio to finish the record, but I'm too busy living the life. I finally know what stardom feels like, and I love it. I've gone a little overboard a few times but, luckily for me, Amy and her friends are well experienced in the field of overindulgence. Divine Light seem to have fallen into the rock music abyss. Their debut album has bombed, and Maxx is headed to rehab. What a mess. I feel sorry for the guys, but I'm too lost in my world to really care.

I'm alone in the unit working on a few new tunes when I hear a knock on the door. I walk down the stairs and see Dani through the glass doors.

"Dani? What are you doing here?"

"Sorry I didn't call first, but you never answer when I do. I got in touch with Rikki, he said you'd be here. Can we talk?"

"Of course, come up." I lock the door behind us and walk up the stairs.

"Wow. This is a cool spot, what is this place?" Dani asks as she looks around the unit.

"Thanks, sorry for the mess. This is where me and my friends hang out. That jam room right there is where Divine Light began. It's my safe place, it's where I come to write and escape for a while. So, what did you want to talk about?"

"I feel like I'm losing you, Rai. You're out a lot, and you're losing focus on your music. I know the single is doing really well, and you're getting a lot of attention, but let's not lose focus on what's important right now, your album."

"I know, I'm sorry. I haven't been totally focused, but I'm having a little fun. I'm in a good place now, I'm happy."

"Weren't you happy before?"

"That's a complicated question. I've always been happy, but this is different. This is my chance to finally do something for me, you know? Like you, you have your own studio, that was your dream and you went for it. You're doing what you love."

"I get it. But, one thing I can tell you is this. It's much harder to see flaws from a distance. The closer you get to something you think is perfect, the more imperfections you'll find. You see me as a studio owner, but what you don't see is all the people I've lost along the way to get here."

"What do you mean?"

"I haven't talked to my family or any of old friends in years. I gave up everything I had to open my studio. I burned bridges and took relationships for granted. In the beginning sure, maybe I was happy, but that didn't last long. I would give anything to get my family and friends back, but I can't, the damage is done."

"I guess I haven't looked at it that way."

"Sometimes we're blinded by our obsessions. I'm sorry to lay this all on you, I just wanted you to know. I don't want you to end up like Maxx, or even worse, part of the infamous twenty-seven club. Let's get back to the music, we're so close to finishing."

I don't know how she knew, but I needed to hear that. Dani's talk was the motivation I needed to get back to the studio. We hop in her car and head back to SubRock.

♫   ♫   ♫

We settle back into our spots, me on my guitar stool, and Dani behind the piano. We play all night and get through all the remaining songs. The only thing left to do is mix and master the tracks. We head into the mixing room and listen.

We're all but done when my phone rings; it's Amy. I motion to Dani that I have to take it, and quickly walk over to the piano and sit on the bench.

"Hey, Aim."

"Hey, Rai, where are you?"

"I'm actually in the studio; I'm finally finishing my album."

"That's so exciting, congratulations. I've never been in a music studio before. Can I come by?"

"I don't know, it's really late."

"Come on, I won't get in the way, I promise."

"Actually, we're pretty much done. Give me a few minutes and we can go grab a drink to celebrate. I'm at SubRock Records in Queen West. Come in like twenty minutes."

"Okay, yay!"

I hang up the phone and walk back into the mixing room. Dani is working her magic on the mixing board; the songs sound amazing. She has her headphones on, so I tap her on her shoulder, breaking her concentration.

"This sounds great."

"It sounds so good, Rai. I'm so proud of you. It's a great record."

"Thanks to you."

"I'm almost done, wanna have a listen?"

"It's okay, it's late, I'm going to get outta here. I trust you."

"Oh, okay. Where are you going?"

"I totally forgot I had plans tonight, I'm super late."

I can feel my phone buzzing in my pocket. I pull it out and read the text message. It's Amy. I walk towards the window to see Amy in the backseat of a black SUV. She rolls down her window and waves.

"Is everything okay?" Dani asks.

"Yeah, everything is fine. A friend of mine is here to pick me up. Do you mind if she comes up? She's never seen a recording studio before."

"A friend?"

"Yeah, a friend; we met at TIFF, she's an actress. Honestly, she's just a friend."

"Okay, but make it quick. I'm in a groove right now, I want to finish."

Amy greets me outsides with a big hug and a kiss on the cheek. I show her around a little, then we make our way into the mixing room.

"Dani, this is Amy Strong, Amy this is Dani. She owns the studio."

"Nice to meet you, Dani. This place is so cool."

"Thank you. Rai tells me you're an actress. Have you been in any movies I would know?"

"I'm not sure, I've been in a few."

"That's cool, where are you from?"

"Originally from San Diego, you?"

"I'm from here. San Diego, eh? I hear it's beautiful over there, except for all those fires. Didn't they have a crazy fire years ago where all those people died? So sad."

Amy glances at me, then turns back to Dani. "There was, yes."

"Thanks so much for today, Dani," I say. "I had an amazing time. I'm so happy with the album. It's perfect. We're gonna go."

I go to give Dani a friendly hug, but she leans in and gives me a kiss on the cheek instead, locking eyes with Amy and making sure she notices.

"Have a good night," Dani says, still staring at Amy.

Amy and I make our way downstairs and into her car.

"Sebastian, to the hotel please."

"I thought we were going for a drink?" I say.

"We are, in my suite."

We reach the Fairmont Royal York Hotel and make our way up to her penthouse suite. I take off my jacket and lay it on the vintage ottoman in the living room. The Royal York is a legendary hotel, right in the heart of Toronto. The room overlooks the CN Tower and the lakeshore. Amy fixes up a couple of drinks. I sit on one of the fancy chairs; it looks better than it is comfortable. She hands me my drink and sits on the chair opposite me.

"That Dani girl, she likes you, I can tell."

"It's not like that. She's a great producer. She's got a great ear and passion for music."

"She's got passion alright, for you. Do you know a lot about her?" Amy asks.

"Why all the Dani questions?"

"I don't trust her. I think Henry is manipulating the program again. He's done it to me before. He takes control of someone in the program, someone you're close to, and uses them as a tool to try and get you out. Does she seem different from the first time you met her?"

"What? You're crazy. Nobody is out to get you, relax. I know Dani, she wouldn't do that."

"Don't you think it's strange that she hasn't heard of me? I don't want to sound arrogant or anything, but my last two movies were box office hits. I'm in every newspaper, on every billboard, you can't turn on the TV without seeing my face."

"Not everyone cares about movie stars, Amy. She's not into that. She's all about music."

"Okay, what about the fire? She said there was a crazy fire in San Diego, years ago. That fire was just two years ago in here, but seventeen years ago in the real world. Explain that?"

What Amy is saying is starting to make sense. Dani has been acting differently around me recently. We talk about different things than we used to, she even looks a little different, her eyes have changed. Something weird is going on.

"Honestly, I have noticed some changes in her recently."

"You see, I knew it. Who do you think it is? Jack? Sam? Henry? It's probably Henry, he's always got something up his sleeve."

"I don't know. Let me do some digging."

Amy puts down her glass and walks towards me. She straddles my legs and wraps her arms around my shoulders. She talks softly while she tickles on my neck with her lips.

"You'll protect me right, Rai? Stay with me in the program, we have it all here. We're doing what we love, we have fame, fortune, and we have each other."

Amy kisses me softly at first, then more sensually to the point where I have to stop her. I grab her hands and hold her back, but I can't resist. Sometimes something you know is wrong, feels so right. Amy is my wrong now, she's my fix.

CHAPTER NINE

Jack paces back and forth in the bedroom hallway while Sam sits at her vanity, applying her eyeshadow.

"Sam, we can't keep hiding like this. The press won't stop until we do something. We've been cooped up in this house for two weeks now. We keep getting letters from the lawyers for Amy's estate, threatening us with subpoenas. I don't know, Sam, this is bad. What are we going to do?"

"Relax, Jack, we'll think of something, we always do."

"What if we just walk in there, yank all the tubes out of her, and pull her out. We'll say we found her on the streets, living under a bridge somewhere all drugged out. She's an actress, that's believable."

"Jack, you've told me a million times, we can't just pull her out, her body can't handle it. And if by some miracle it does, who knows what she'll do to herself. Then what? It'll be our fault. Henry has to get her out on her terms, it must be her decision."

"Well then, how do you suppose we do that?"

Jack sits next to Sam while she stares at herself in the mirror. She grabs her brush and calmy strokes her hair as she lays out her plan.

"First, we need to find Henry. Then, we tell him to make things a little more uncomfortable for Amy in the program. She doesn't want to leave because she has everything she wants in there. It's time for us to start taking things away."

"Like what?" Jack asks.

"What if there's a second fire? Natural disasters are an unfortunate reoccurring phenomenon, you know. We take her out the same way we got her in, we take out her family."

"We can't, Sam, that's too much. There has to be a better way. That will destroy her."

"We have to. You know it's the only way she'll come out. Besides, it's just a dream world, Jack, don't get so emotional. She'll be fine. But we need Henry. Where is he?"

"I don't know, I can't get hold of him. But one thing I do know is Henry has a soft spot for Amy. He'll never do it unless we force his hand. Let me handle Henry, I know who to call."

♫   ♫   ♫

Henry pulls Rachyl from her session. He gently disconnects her from the headset and gives her a moment to recover.

"Rachyl, are you okay? You did great."

"Yeah, I'm okay. I felt like it was going well until that Amy girl showed up. I was really getting to him. He was listening and trusting me. I know I was convincing him to come back. She got me all frazzled. Is that really Amy Strong? Is she alive?"

"Yes, it's her. They're in there together; it's a long story. We must save them both before Jack and Sam get here. They don't care about them, they just want the problems to go away and the show to go on. I just hope Amy didn't catch what you said about the fire."

"I know, after I said it, I realized my mistake."

"It's okay, I don't think she caught it. Go home and get some sleep, it's almost morning. Jack and Sam will be here any minute. You did great; Rai misses you guys, he'll come back. Try not to worry too much. I'll get him out."

"Henry, please, bring him back."

"I will."

Rachyl makes her way back home. She walks in the door and immediately falls into the comforting arms of June. The kids are asleep, and June has a mug of warm coffee waiting for her.

"What happened, Rach? Is Rai okay?"

"I can't believe it. He's hooked up to this machine; they're using a computer program to access his memories. It's crazy, June."

"Slow down. What are you talking about? Is that even possible?"

"I don't know how, but it is possible. I was in it."

"What do you mean?"

"The show is actually a virtual world happening in Rai's mind. When I got there, Henry was tied up to his desk. He said that Rai drugged him, tied him up, and somehow went into the program himself. He thinks Rai might be addicted to his life in the program. Next thing I know he's hooking me up and I'm in this program as this Dani girl. I think I made it worse. It's bad, June. I'm so scared."

"It's okay. If there's one thing I know, it's that Rai loves you and the kids more than anything in the world. He'll find a way out. I know he will."

"This is all just so crazy, I can't believe this is happening. I just wanted him to be happy, you know. I thought he would go there, tell his story, play some of his songs, and that would be it. I know he misses playing music. He's always putting other people first, he deserved this opportunity. But I never thought it would be like this, nothing like this."

"I know Rach, I'm scared too. But it's Rai we're talking about, I know he'll come back. Come on, let's stay positive. We should watch the new *Remarkable* episode from last night. I recorded it, let's see what's happening." June grabs the remote and searches for the episode.

♫   ♫   ♫

Jack makes his way down the elevator to the Remarkable chambers and heads straight for Henry's office. He finds him glued to his computer screen.

"Henry! What is hell is going on? Where have you been and why haven't you been answering my calls?"

"I'm sorry, Jack, I've been in the program trying to get Amy out, then I ran into a little problem. Rai has lost it; he and Amy are working together now. He gassed me, tied me up, and went into the program himself. I'm working on a solution, I just need a little more time."

"What? That's it! This has gone too far. Your time is up, Sam and I are taking over now. Amy is coming out today, we're going to smoke her out. Program a fire in her parents' neighborhood; I want her family and friends gone."

"I can't do that. It's not right. She doesn't deserve that. You don't know how she's going to react."

"Listen, Henry, we're not going to lose everything we have because you feel bad for them. They were nobodies before we put them in your little dream world and gave them their dreams back. Do it, now."

"I won't do that to her."

"We were afraid you might say that. Sam, bring him in."

Sam walks into Henry's office. With her is a man. Tall and in full uniform, the officer stands with his chest out and his hands crossed in front of him.

"Henry, this is Detective Wallace, a friend of ours. He also happens to be the lead in the Amy Strong investigation. His daughter, Sarah, is a huge fan of the show, and guess what? She's going to be our next feature artist, isn't that fantastic? Detective Wallace, this is Henry Strat."

"Mr. Strat, you are under arrest for the abduction of Amy Strong. With the cooperation of Mr. and Mrs. Cranney, new security video recordings have surfaced of you tending to the machines in her hidden chamber. I've gathered enough irrefutable evidence here that will no doubt be very harmful for you in a court of law."

"Wait, are you blackmailing me?" Henry asks.

"I'm just simply stating the facts, Mr. Strat," Detective Wallace says as he displays his handcuffs and makes his way toward Henry. Henry stands up and tries to shove his hands away, but the detective is too strong.

"It doesn't have to be this way, Henry," says Sam. "Just do what we ask, program the fire and all this will go away. Don't be stupid, take the deal."

"I always knew you two were evil, but this is just vile."
Henry sits back in his chair and logs into the program.

They watch over him as he programs the devastation. The
death that Henry orchestrates is killing him just as much as Amy's
family. Every press of the keyboard is like a knife to his heart.

"There, it's done. Are you happy now?"

"We'll be happy when Amy and Rai are out, and Sam and I
can get some peace and quiet," Jack says.

"What's the matter, life in the public eye isn't so easy, is it?"
Henry says.

In a flash, Jack punches Henry square in the jaw. Henry
swirls in his chair and falls to the ground. Detective Wallace jumps
in and holds Jack back. "Enough, Jack, it's over. Come on, show me
the girl."

♫   ♫   ♫

Life in the program is perfect, well, almost perfect. I'm doing what I
love and living like a king. The only things missing are Rachyl and
the kids, but even those thoughts are beginning to fade. I can see
why Amy wants to stay here forever. Amy and I are living together;
we love this hotel suite so much that we've booked it indefinitely.
My album comes out today. Dani said there's a huge pre-order list,
but I'm still nervous.

Amy usually starts her morning with a coffee and a call to
her mom back home. She woke up before I did, and has been trying
all morning, but no answer. She tries her friends, but no answer still.

"Is everything okay, Aim?" I ask.

"I don't know. It's strange that no one is answering today. I know it's probably fine, but I have a bad feeling."

"I'm sure they're all just busy; people don't just stand by their phones waiting for people to call them."

"I know, but all of them?"

"Did you leave messages?"

"Yeah."

"Then don't worry, they'll call you back. Come on, I'll make you some breakfast."

I head to the little hotel kitchenette to make my world-famous cheesy eggs. Amy makes her way to the table and pours herself some orange juice. Finally, her cell phone rings. She reaches for it, but I stop her.

"Hey, it can wait. Let's just enjoy our breakfast for ten minutes. I told you, everything is fine, they'll leave a message."

"I can't, Rai, I'm sorry. It's a strange number, I have to answer it."

Amy flips open her phone and answers the call. She walks toward the bedroom for some privacy. I put a fork full of cheesy eggs onto my toast and take a huge bite. I reach for the remote and turn on the TV. My eyes focus on the screen as my mouth stops chewing. I flip through the channels to make sure it's real; it's on every channel.
Amy walks in the room and drops to the floor with a deafening scream. I go over and wrap my arms around her. Her body is limp, and she's inconsolable.

"What happened? Who was it?"

"It was the hospital in San Diego. There was a fire. My parents, they're gone. It happened again. I can't believe he would do this to me."

As I comfort Amy, I am furious. Virtual or not, this is war. I know Sam and Jack are involved, but only Henry can program something like this. He must have figured out a way to get free. I call out for Henry to enter the program, I know he's watching.

"Henry, meet me in the lobby."

I walk Amy back to bed, the eggs will have to wait. I quickly get dressed and then give her a kiss on the forehead. I know they're watching, so I sneak my free arm under the bed and snatch the revolver that she keeps for protection. I quickly tuck it under my shirt and adjust my clothes. We both know what has to be done. I would have never thought I could do something like this, but my mind is fueled with rage.

The elevator doors open, and I can see Henry waiting outside in front of the lobby doors, leaning against his car. I take a deep breath and confront him.

"You made it," I say, trying to be casual.

"I did. No thanks to you. What were you thinking, Rai? Why would you do that to me?"

"I had to, I knew you wouldn't understand. My life is perfect in here, and I plan to keep it that way."

"Rai, stop it. You know this isn't real. You sound just as crazy as Amy right now, but worse, you have a family, she doesn't."

"Don't talk about Amy after what you did to her. How could you do that to her, after all she's been through?"

"I had nothing to do with that."

My palms are sweating, and my legs are weak. I'm not as confident as I thought. I realize I don't have a plan of how to do this. There are way too many people around; I can't just shoot him here. I think on my feet and try to get him to follow me.

"Really? We know you're the only one who can program something like that. How dumb do you think we are?"

"Okay fine, look, not everything is under my control. Sam and Jack are powerful people, with powerful connections. They're taking over; I had to do it."

"Why don't you come up and explain that to Amy; she's devastated."

Henry agrees and turns to park his car. I watch closely as he walks back towards the hotel, making sure he's alone. He cautiously walks through the revolving glass doors and follows me up to the suite. I can barely stand the sight of him as we silently wait for the elevator doors to open. I slip my keycard into the slot, and, after a faint beep, I push the suite door open. Amy has made her way to the couch; she's wearing her oversized sunglasses and has made herself a drink. She sees Henry but doesn't move an inch.

"Amy, I'm so sorry, I had no choice. They blackmailed me. The cops were there, they were going to throw me in jail. Sam and Jack are dangerous; I don't know what they're capable of doing. You have to believe me, I'm sorry."

As Henry is speaking, I grab the revolver from my belt and point it at him. As I pull the gun hammer back, he hears the click and looks back at me. He lunges for the gun and we struggle on the ground for what seems like hours but is only seconds in real time. He has his hand on the gun, as do I, but it's hard to tell who is in control. The gun slips from our grasp and we begin to deliver alternating blows, each landing fierce punches to the body and face. Henry lands a deafening blow to the side of my face, my ears ring, and my body retracts. Henry's punches suddenly stop, and his body goes limp. I begin to realize, it wasn't a punch that buzzed my ears, it was the gun.

Amy is standing over us, holding the revolver with both her hands, and a look of crazed joy on her face. A small stream of smoke billows from the barrel as the buzzing in my ears begins to subside. I've never heard a gun fire up close before. It's much more powerful then I imagined.

"Amy, put the gun down, it's over."

Amy slowly lowers the gun and extends her hand to help me up. We both look down at Henry and notice something extraordinary happening. His body is slowly pixelating and fading, until only his clothes remain. Amy is taking this situation much better than I am; I have a feeling this is not her first time. Amy's emotions turn cold as she turns to leave and retreats to the bedroom. Losing people you love can change a person; everyone has a dark side, and for the first time, I'm beginning to see Amy's.

Like the flick of a switch, my mind begins to clear. This has gone too far; it's time for me to go home. Once Amy is out of sight, I frantically look for Henry's car keys. I know the car has the ability to travel in and out of the program, I just need to figure out how. I find the keys, slip out the door, and head for Henry's car.

As soon as I unlock the door and sit down in the driver's seat, the engine starts up. Screens are opening, and lights are flashing all around me. I have no idea where to begin. My phone starts ringing; it's Amy, she's noticed I've left. I answer the phone and try to keep as calm as possible.

"Amy, sorry, I had to get some air and clear my head."

"Rai, it had to be done, now we can live the life we've always wanted. I thought this is what you wanted? That's why you grabbed the gun, isn't it?"

"I know, but I've never done anything like that before, I just need some time to calm down."

"I understand, take your time, come home when you're ready."

I hang up and turn my attention back to the car. The only thing that looks familiar to me is the navigation device. Henry used it to find his garage on my first night in the program. I press a few buttons and see an option that reads "Home." I press it, and instantly the car starts moving. I put my hands on the wheel and hope for the best.

CHAPTER TEN

Henry's body jumps in the chamber the moment the bullet enters his body. The machine lights up and emergency alarms sound as he goes into shock. Jack hears the warnings and springs into action. He immobilizes Henry's body and quickly reads his levels; his blood pressure is dangerously low. Jack frantically hooks up more fluids to regulate the pressure, then fills a syringe with a heavy dose of Dopamine to bring his levels back up. Once he inserts the Dopamine, the alerts begin to subside. Jack takes a deep breath; he can't lose Henry, not now. Sam comes running in from her office.

"I saw everything, I was watching live, she shot him. She's completely lost it now. It's perfect. Amy Strong is a murderer, imagine the ratings. We can edit this flawlessly. Two worlds collide, Rai Starr and Amy Strong join forces to avenge her parents' killer. We can make Henry the fire starter. This is our finale show, the perfect ending." Sam smiles ear to ear as she shares her vison.

"But how do we explain Amy being on the show?" Jack asks.

"We tell the press she came back to us, she showed up at our door after life on the streets. We brought her in and gave her the help she needs. I'm working on the official press release right now."

"That's brilliant."

"It gets better, Jack, listen to this. Henry was using Rachyl to get Rai out. She's here, she's Dani!"

"Wow, Henry, you sneak. What do we do now?"

"As far as I see it, there is only one way out. It's time for Rai to join his heroes; every legend must have a tragic ending. He's coming out, I'll be there when he does. You make sure Henry comes out of this alive so Wallace can charge him. Then, we need to get rid of Rachyl; she knows too much, pull her."

♫　　♫　　♫

I wake up with Sam Cranney standing over me. I'm not sure what she knows, but she never comes into the chamber rooms. Something's wrong.

"Rai, are you alright? We saw what Amy did, she's lost it. Don't you worry, we know it's not your fault."

"I tried to stop her but she's relentless. She's never going to leave the program."

"It's alright, you don't have to worry about that anymore, we'll take it from here. Listen, there's something I have to tell you. There's been an accident. I don't know how to say this."

"What is it? Tell me."

"It's Rachyl; she's in the hospital."

"What happened? Is it serious?"

"She was driving home from work when some deranged fan spotted her at a red light. The fan started following her and Rachyl sped up to try and get away from her. She lost control of the car and rolled into a ditch. She's in the ICU at Sunnybrook Hospital. She's stable, but it's bad."

I can hear the words, but my mind and body are numb. I sit in silence, frozen with fear. It's my fault. All of this is my fault. I feel an intense combination of panic, sadness, and fury. I know time moves differently in the program, but I just left. One thing I know for sure, if Rachyl is hurt, June will be there. I have to call her.

"I have to see her, Sam, take me to the hospital, please."

"Of course, I'll have a driver ready when you are."

"Thank you; give me a second to get dressed."

Sam leaves and I call June to see how bad it really is; she won't lie to me. Something isn't right, I can feel it in my bones. June picks up quickly and sounds oddly casual considering the situation.

"Hey, Rai."

"Oh my god, June, is she okay?"

"Who?"

"Rachyl!"

"Rai, you're freaking me out. I'm at work, did something happen? I talked to her this morning, she was fine."

I pause to gather my thoughts. I try to calm June down before she really freaks out, while I try and figure this out.

"I just can't get a hold of her. You know how I freak out sometimes. Don't worry, I'm sure she just forgot her phone or something. Did she say where she was going today?"

"Well, I'm not supposed to tell you this, but we were all just so scared that you weren't going to come out. She spoke to Henry and went to the Remarkable building to try and help you. I'm so happy you're out, you scared me for a second, but I knew you'd do the right thing."

"Thanks, June, I'm sure she's here somewhere. I'm at the Reckless building. I'll let you know when I find her."

I hang up the phone and think. If Rachyl is hidden somewhere in this building, I'll never find her. Maybe she's still in the program looking for me. I know it will be easier to find her in the program. The moment I open the door, Sam is standing there, face-to-face with me.

"Are you ready to go? The car's waiting outside."

I peer outside and see a car parked with two large men waiting for me. I don't think it takes two people to drive someone to the hospital. I know if I get in that car, I might not ever be coming back.

"Yes, but before we do, I need to tell you something."

"What is it?" Sam asks.

"I can't do this anymore. Being on this show isn't worth the safety of my family. But I don't feel right just quitting. Let me go in, right now, one last time to finish the show and fulfill my contract. It will take just a few minutes. When I'm done, I'll go straight to Rachyl, the show will be done, and all this will be behind us."

Sam looks at me intently. She takes a second, looks away, and nods her head. "Okay, Rai, you go back in there and finish up, just remember, we will be watching."

I jump back into the chamber and quickly prepare for entry into the program. I search for Dani's location and enter the codes. I take a deep breath, close my eyes, and hit the switch.

♫　　　♫　　　♫

Henry recovers from the shock of his program death and gradually opens his eyes in his chamber. He holds the spot where the bullet entered his body. He knows he's alive, but the pain is overwhelming. He can see Jack attending to his vitals, while Detective Wallace stands guard outside the hall. Jack notices Henry's eyes opening.

"Henry, when are you going to give up? Just let her go. You love her, don't you? I told you, never get involved with a featured artist, it will inevitably lead to trouble."

"I can't let her go knowing what I did to her, I'm not like you."

"Oh, Henry, but you are like me. You cash your cheques and play with all these toys I buy you, don't you? Need I remind you, you created this world."

"I may have created this world, but it's you two who poisoned it. It's you two who bribed the FCC, and it's you two who decided to hide Amy's body when she wouldn't come out."

"That's right, and we'll do the same to Rai and Rachyl because that's life, Henry. We do what we have to do. It's kill or be killed, only the strong survive, whatever saying you want to use, that's reality."

"That's not my reality, Jack, we all create our own reality. We should have come clean to begin with and none of this would have happened."

"You know what, maybe you held her hostage here because you're madly in love with her. Maybe you used the program to kidnap her so you could have Amy all to yourself. Did you hear that, Detective Wallace?" Jack looks back to see an empty hallway where Wallace was standing.

Just then, Sam walks in and whispers in Jacks ear, "Rai's going back in, this is our chance. Did you unplug Rachyl?"

"Not yet."

"You take care of Rachyl, I'll take care of Rai." Sam and Jack leave Henry to recover and head their separate ways.

Jack enters Rachyl's chamber and quickly reaches for the power cord.

"I wouldn't touch that if I were you. You already admitted to two crimes, I wouldn't add murder to your sentence." Wallace's deep voice echoes in the chamber. Detective Wallace directs two agents to handcuff Jack.

"Wallace, what are you talking about? We have a deal."

"I don't think so. You did get one thing right, I am on the Amy Smart case, but on the right side. Detective Wallace FBI. You're under arrest. By the way, my daughter hates your show."

♫ ♫ ♫

Sam reaches Rai's chamber and turns on the computer to see where he is, and what he's doing. The program locates Rai at Amy's apartment. Sam smirks: she's anxious to see how this will unfold.

As the feed begins, Sam sees Rai on a balcony having a heated argument with Amy. She watches as Amy runs towards Rai in anger; this is the moment she's been waiting for. Just as Amy reaches Rai, the feed cuts out. Sam looks up and sees Wallace holding the unplugged video cables in his hands, with Jack in handcuffs behind him. He flashes his FBI badge.

"It's over, Sam. Jack has confessed to everything. Get on your feet, put your hands on your head, and walk towards me, slowly."

Sam looks at Jack and realizes the severity of the situation. She turns to Wallace.

"No, no, you've got it all wrong. It's all fake, it's just a television show. Everyone is here, alive, and well. Please, Wallace."

"That's for the judge to decide." Wallace grabs each of her hands and handcuffs her.

"You can't do this! Do you know who I am? Jack! Say something!"

"He's said enough," Wallace says.

"No! I thought he was your friend, Jack! Do something!" Sam says, kicking and screaming, as Wallace walks her and Jack out of the building and into the back of a black unmarked sedan.

♪   ♪   ♪

I enter the program right where I exited, looking up at the endless balconies from the hotel parking lot below. I hope Dani is inside, but I also don't. I know what Amy is capable of; if Dani is in there, she's in trouble. I knock on the door, no response. I knock louder until finally, the door slowly opens and Amy is staring at me.

"Rai, that was a long walk. We've had a visitor since you've been gone."

"Where is she, Amy? Where's Dani?"

"You mean Rachyl? Don't worry, she's in the bedroom, she's safe, for now. She told me what Henry's been up to. So, what's it going to be, Rai? An ordinary, dull, boring, and unfulfilling life or everything you've ever wanted, including me?"

I run into the bedroom, but Dani is nowhere to be seen. The balcony door is open, the curtains sway from the breeze outside. I pull back the curtains and walk onto the balcony. I notice a rope tied to the railing, I look over and see Dani tied at the wrists, legs dangling, hanging over the railing hundreds of feet from the ground. Her face is swollen and bloody. Her eyes open wide as she sees me. Her body is swinging as she screams desperately for help.

Amy slowly walks behind me with a look of madness in her eyes. "There's a knife on the chair beside you; all you have to do is cut that rope and it's me and you, forever."

"Amy, please, this has gone too far. I'm pulling her up, let's talk about this."

"You make one move towards that rope and I'll push you over. I thought you were finally realizing that all you've ever dreamed is here, in this program."

"I've realized that what I already have is more important to me than any dream."

"She doesn't understand you like I do. We're artists, Rai, we have a gift, people adore us. We'll figure out a way to stay here forever. This is where we belong, Rai, this is our destiny."

"She does understand me, Amy, that's why she's here, that's why she's fighting for me. You've been deceived by the fame, you don't know what's real anymore. It's love, Amy, that's the dream, it's always been love. You don't have to be rich, or famous, or popular to have it, it's out there for all of us to find. I know you lost your family and you feel like you're all alone, but you're not. There are people in the real world who love and adore you, you just have to let them in."

Amy takes a second to take in what I've said. She smiles and begins to walk towards me.

"You know what, Rai, maybe you're right. Maybe there is someone for me in the real world. But it's too bad I'll never get the chance to find out, and neither will you."

Amy rushes towards me with her arms out. Just as her palms are about to reach my chest, I bend down and propel her over the railing with my shoulder. She desperately grabs for Dani's ankles on the way down and tries to pull her down with her. I reach for the rope and hold on as hard as I can. Amy's fingers begin to slip; she loses her grip and her body plummets to the ground below. I pull on the rope as hard as I can and pull Dani back over the railing to safety. I grab the knife from the chair and cut her free. We reach for each other and share an unforgettable kiss.

"You came back to save me."

"It's always been you, Rachyl. I've realized that my music was never destined for fame, it was all to find you."

♫   ♫   ♫

The television screen fades to black as the credits begin to scroll across the screen. Rachyl and I are curled up on the couch, under a blanket, totally immersed in the last episode of *Remarkable*.

"Wow, I can't believe you actually kissed that psycho Amy girl," Rachyl says.

"That's what you took away from all of that?"

Rachyl and I share a bottle of wine and reminisce. Our connection has never been stronger, and we owe it all to *Remarkable*. As powerful as fame can be, it can never replace true love. With Rachyl by my side, Nellie and Aly tucked safely in their beds, I am living my dream and will be, evermore.

♫   ♫   ♫

"Amy, it's okay, you're okay. It's me, Henry, I'm here. Try not to move so much, your body is weak. You're in the hospital, take it slow." Henry holds Amy's hand.

He's been by her side since she's been out of the program. She'd been in so long that her body took two weeks to heal. She's been in an induced coma and is finally coming to.

Amy begins to weep as she realizes all that she's done. Since her parents' passing, she's been running away from reality, only to face it here. She remembers her early acting years, how the love of film drove her, not the fame and riches. She misses the love of family and friends. But all that's left is the aftermath of stardom. She wonders what will drive her ambitions now, what's left to live for. She raises her arm and points to a stack of boxes lying on the floor beside her.

"Henry, what is this?"

Henry smiles. "These are for you." He opens a box, reaches for an envelope, and opens it. He begins to read one of the thousands of letters fans have written to Amy, each one containing personal stories of heartache, and telling Amy how she has inspired them to carry on and reach for their dreams.

"You see, Amy, you are loved." Amy takes the letter from Henry's hand and reads it. She hugs the letter and finally realizes she does have a reason to live.

"Amy, they believe in you, like I believe in you, always."

Henry's words bring Amy back to the program, remembering what Eric would always say whenever she was down. She realizes it was Henry all along. Every time he said I believe in you, what he really meant was, I love you. She reaches in for a kiss and whispers,

"I love you too."

♫   ♫   ♫

I enter the hospital room with a bouquet of gerbera daisies. I'm happy to see Henry by Amy's side, I was hoping to see him here.

"Well, isn't this a sight. I knew you two would be great together. These are for you. How are you feeling, Amy?"

"Thank you. I'm feeling much better, I'm just really tired. I never thought I'd say this but, thank you for throwing me off that balcony, Rai, it saved my life."

"It was my pleasure," I say with a chuckle. "I'm just grateful we're out. Do you mind if I speak to Henry?"

"I don't mind, thanks for coming, it means a lot to me."

"Of course, wouldn't miss it for the world. I'll see you when you get outta here, get better soon."

Henry and I leave the room and let Amy rest. We sit in the waiting room and talk.

"Hey, now that this is all over, I'm sorry I didn't listen to you. I should have just focused on the music and got out. But everything got crazy and I lost control."

"I'm sorry too. I know the program is powerful, I never meant it to hurt anybody. I just wanted to help people find peace. I didn't calculate how dangerous fame can be. I'm glad it's all over and everyone is safe. I'm shutting down the program, for good."

"Before you do, can I ask you for a favor?"

"No, please, Rai, no more."

"It's not like that. I know it's not real, but there's one more thing I have to do."

♪   ♪   ♪

I open my eyes one last time in the program and find myself walking towards The Farm Drug Rehab Centre. It's eerily quiet as I walk up the cobblestone steps lined with miniature evergreen trees. I open the door and walk to the front desk.

"Hello, I'm here to see Maxx Sallen."

"Oh my god, you're Rai Starr, right? My son is a huge fan. He plays that song, *Exit Sign*, all day."

"That's nice to hear, thank you."

"Can I get your autograph? My son is going to flip out."

"No problem, right after I speak to my friend, if you don't mind."

"Of course, I'm sorry, right this way."

She leads me down a hallway which leads to an outside courtyard. I see Maxx sitting on a wooden bench, by himself, playing his acoustic guitar. I walk up behind him and say,

"Sounds good. Are you working on something new?"

Maxx looks up at me and says, "Not much else to do. What are you doing here? Last I heard, you were a hotshot solo artist dating a Hollywood actress."

"Yeah, but yet I'm here talking to you. Our friendship is more important to me than any of that. I'm sorry I left the band."

"You don't know what that did to me, man. I felt abandoned, then I had to lead the band, that's a lot of pressure. But I did it, and it worked, we were huge. Then it just got crazy, I needed something to take the edge off, and now I'm here."

"I know the feeling, Maxx. I've been there. It's fame, it takes a hold of you, and it's hard to get free. At the end of the day, after all the riches and spoils, its family and friendship that's important. That's why I'm here. I miss you dude. I miss just hanging out and playing music, for us."

"I miss it too, brother. But you have your hit record now, your famous girlfriend, we can't just go back to how it used to be."

"You've been in here for a while, you haven't heard. I'm done with music and with Amy. I heard my songs on the radio and people liked it, that's all I ever needed. And Amy, well let's just say we had a falling out. When you're better, come find me, let's hang out."

"I'd like that. I'm glad you came, wait, before you leave, what do you think of this riff?"

Maxx and I play for a little while, just like old times. He plays his guitar, and I add some vocal melodies to the music. Before I leave, we share a hug, and a promise that we'll never let music get in the way of our friendship.

♫   ♫   ♫

Jack and Sam Cranney were convicted of several criminal offences, in the areas of business fraud and abduction. After the conclusion of Rai's season, *Remarkable* was taken off the air. The season finale was the most watched reality show episode of all time.

♫   ♫   ♫

Amy and Henry eventually got married and started a family. They launched a foundation that helps young people deal with the death of family members. Henry built a new form of memory-based virtual reality where people can converse with and say goodbye to their deceased family and friends.

♫   ♫   ♫

So, I ask you, would you give up all you have to go back and live the life you've always dreamed?

Rai Starr
SONG LYRICS

"Bad ones"

If I fall into your emptiness,
will you dive after me
all I need is your empathy,
and someone to want me
even though I was unprepared,
or just too blind to see
you were all you were meant to be,
but just a friend to me

Can it be another day
Can it be another day

I always thought that I was good enough,
but good isn't what she needs
they always end up with the bad ones,
the ones that hurt and cheat
maybe I'm not what I thought I was,
please explain to me
wasn't I the one who had it all,
the way you wanted me

    -Rai Starr

"Been through"

I've seen it all again this year
something's wrong, it felt so real
I walked into your pain,
did you know I feel the same
lives have changed in your mind
a helping hand is hard to find

I'm around, I'll be there when you're down
let me know how you feel
cause your life is all that's real

I was there to meet your fate
was I there a bit too late
take the love inside of me
a little help is all you need
let it lay in your past
let your mind and soul relax

I'll provide, what you need to know in time
let your mind set at ease
cause your life is all that's real

        -Rai Starr

"Far away eyes"

I see my life with far away eyes,
to focus through the lies and truths
beat them down but they break through,
to become who they were meant to
a mind, a way, and all of your dreams,
together sung in sweet harmony
fight your fears to feed your drive,
and take the risks to live your life

The shadows are always hiding,
come out from under your chains
excuses are there if you're losing,
but I want to win

Once you're there your mind is clear
you've become who you were meant to
the times were hard, the fight was long
you found the strength to carry on
looking back to all that was
all your hills and holes in walls
it's all your life in all its faults
all connected to who you are

　　　-Rai Starr

"I must be crazy"

It's twelve o'clock, on the dot,
I better get down to my spot
I see your name across the screen, will I answer
what will I do, what will I say,
I wonder why she talks to me
could it be, its plain to see, I've fallen for you

This is war, I can't win
I'll feel the pain again
this is war, I can't win
unless I, unless I, leave again

The more I talk to you all day,
the more I know you're right for me
I better get out while I can before I fall down
do you feel the way I feel, did we have something real
a kiss is all I really need
I must be crazy

 -Rai Starr

"I'll try to feel alive"

If I did my time again,
would I change my fate again
I never seem to feel alright, even if I do it right
I'm writing down my past again,
trying to fix my head again
even when I feel alright, I always find a way,
a way to make it grey
if I needed you to carry me, what if I said no,
what if I won't go

I'll try, I'll try,
I'll try to feel alive

Trying to find someone like you,
someone to get my mind off you
will you understand my signs, even when you seem so blind
do I have to change my ways,
changing ways makes me complain
even when I feel alright, I always find a way,
a way to make it grey
if you needed me to carry you, what if I said no,
what if I won't go

    -Rai Starr

"Love, thoughts and knots"

Will I ever feel like everyone else
something's wrong inside me, I can't figure it out
look inside me again to find out why
why I feel this way, it's just not right

I guess I can't complain, we must be all the same
we all have or faults,
love, thoughts, and knots
I need something more, searching for a cure
for someone I am not,
love, thoughts, and knots

Another chapter in my miserable life
nothing changed around me, it's still not right
is there a place to run to, somewhere a place to hide
I'll take my vision with me, and head on out

-Rai Starr

"Poor suffering me"

I've been down and out, I've been down on my knees,
slave to my disease
you kept standing there, you kept standing by my side,
where I need you to be

I'll get out, but my head just won't let it be
I'll get out, but my head just won't let me leave

Sitting by myself, watching my room melt
thinking about my pain
murdered by my past, how long will I last
poor suffering me

So what can I eat, can I eat what's in me,
eat what's ailing me
I can't go nowhere, I've been trapped here for years,
waiting for my release

    -Rai Starr

"Exit Sign"

If I stood beneath an exit sign, would you walk through me
enter by my better side to see, anything you need
an open road with endless rows can't lead, the right way
back to you

I'm lost again, I can't pretend
you'll find me there, turn back again
and meet me here

if I could, I would apologize for everything I've done
sorry words will only magnify, the mess that I'm in
a hundred strands of trusting hands can't hold the weight of
losing you

I'm lost again, I can't pretend
you'll find me there, turn back again
and meet me here

    -Rai Starr

"Trapped"

It's amazing that you talk to me
it's alright, that you care
I'll lift your pain up on my shoulders,
and carry it away

It's amazing when you look at me
it's alright, that you stare
I'll put your face on all my worries,
and carry them away

I'm trapped in your net, you set me up
you entered my life to leave
you say no, but I can't believe
you exit, I'm left to bleed

It's amazing that you're in love with me
it's alright, that you're scared
I know you'll leave me in your shadow,
never to return

It's amazing that I've lost my will
but it's alright, no one cares
I'll live my life like no one's watching,
and live with my disease

-Rai Starr

"Heaven's not awake"

You are not alone, but there is no one with you
heaven's not awake, waiting for you
I can't understand, why there's no one with you
counting my mistakes, waiting for you

Bring a little light, so I can see my ending
something to believe, waiting for you
how long will I wait, for someone to come with me
heaven's not awake, waiting for you

Can it be, the memory, is still there
run your fingers through your hair
suddenly, and finally, I don't care
all I know is you're not there
heaven's still a dream to me
give me something to believe

-Rai Starr

Thank You

There are many people to thank, too many to list here. First and foremost, thank you to my beautiful wife Tori and wonderful children Nellie and Alyssa. Without you in my life, there are no words. To my extraordinary friends and extended family, thank you for believing in me and pushing me through my many doubts and fears. Lastly, thank you to all the people, things, views, tastes, smells, and sounds that inspire me every day. You are all my superpower.

Author's Bio

Raimo Strangis is a fiction writer from Toronto, Canada. Aside from writing, Raimo is a Red Seal Certified Chef and accomplished songwriter. His children's novel, *The Kingdom of Grape*, received high praise for its charm, wit, and adventure. His latest novel, *With Little Means*, is his first venture into the young adult fiction genre in hopes to grow with his maturing audience.

Manufactured by Amazon.ca
Bolton, ON

18205741R00085